Where Pirates Go to Die

IE Castellano

Where Pirates Go to Die

Cover by JosDCreations
http://JosDCreations.com

Laurel Highlands Publishing
Mount Pleasant, PA
USA

http://LaurelHighlandsPublishing.com

ISBN-13: 978-1-941087-13-8
ISBN-10: 1941087132

This book is a work of fiction. Names, characters, places, and incidents either are products of the author's imagination or are used fictitiously. Any resemblance to actual persons, living or dead, events, or locales is entirely coincidental.

For the Space Pirate in all of us

Chapter 1

In the darkness, she waited. Her lumpy cot in the four-by-nine cell was only temporary. Through the rectangular opening in the locked door, she listened to the prison guards finish their lights-out rounds. Nighttime was imposed upon them, but she had no intention of sleeping. She knew they would come for her. Enough time had passed since her arrest.

A loud boom shook her cell. Jumping off her cot, she stood with her back to the wall. Light flashed through the small opening in her door. A second boom jarred open the cell door. She smiled.

Prying open her door, she escaped into the chaos. Her dark eyes quickly found the small opening in the prison's wall. Without hesitation, she slipped through the crack.

Her ears discerned the faint, but distinct, hum she knew well over the sounds of the prison break sirens. She ran towards the hum inside the dark gap between the walls that separated Torquor Prison from the vacuum of space.

When her feet found the open hatch, she climbed down metal rungs. At the bottom, dim light greeted her. She knew the metal corridors well and picked her route.

Her chosen corridor brought her to a room with a large view of the vast emptiness of the space quadrant. Two people, a man and a woman, watched screens from their respective seats.

"Are we ready?" she asked them.

"Captain," they both said with smiles.

"We're waiting for, never mind, the hatch has been closed," said the man.

A woman ran into the bridge. "All connections severed," she said. "Make haste. Other ships are coming this way."

The Captain sat in her chair as the other three braced themselves.

"Nitrobooster injected," said a woman. "Hold on to your seats."

The ship bolted through space. White dots became blurs. The Captain saw a large orange wispy blob ahead of them.

"Cut the engines as soon as we enter the Milky Nebula," she told them.

"Yes, Captain," they answered.

Seconds later, they had entered what resembled the center of an orange creamsicle. The ship stopped humming.

"Captain," said one of the women, "we need to make sure your tracker scrambled properly."

The Captain nodded before saying, "Set the timer. Be ready to go when it goes off, not a second later." She rose from her seat.

A flash of nebula lighting streaked through the orange.

"Captain!" a man yelled from the corridor. A burly man entered the bridge, restraining another man wearing a prison uniform. "Found a stowaway. What should we do with him?"

Another flash lit the ship's bridge. She studied the man. Gray streaked his light hair. Lines forked at the corner of his eyes. His beige uniform draped over his unintimidating medium build was as dirty as hers. "You have a name?" she asked.

"Lorne," he answered.

"Well, Lorne, this is your lucky day. You have successfully escaped from Torquor Prison." She smiled. "It was smart to follow me. Unlike other ships, we won't turn you in or expunge you into space. However, we can't just let you off at the next port. You owe us for breaking you out. You understand this don't you?"

Lorne nodded.

"Since I'm not an unreasonable person, I'll let you work off your debt to us on my ship. Besides, every Pirate ship can use another criminal."

"I'm not a criminal," Lorne stated.

The Captain laughed. "You may not think you are a criminal, but someone on the Milky Way Circle believes you to be very dangerous. Not just anyone is incarcerated in Torquor Prison. A maximum security prison floating in the middle of nowhere space is reserved for only the most dangerous criminals." Another streak of lightning lightened the orange. "Tell you what, you don't ask and neither will I. After you have repaid your debt, you are free to go and enjoy whatever freedom a fugitive can have. Do you agree to these terms?"

"Yes," said Lorne.

The man restraining him let go.

"Good. I am Naria, Captain of this fine ship. My first mate is Wretch," she indicated the woman on her right. "That is Gorm. He is copilot and a mechanical genius. Our security expert and prison break mastermind is Pistol. You can thank her later. Behind you is Bob; he will assign you a job. Welcome to the Tigerlily."

Lorne followed Bob through metal corridors. He was relieved to be free. Rumors circulated that someone in the prison was in place to constantly beat the sense into him. He did not know how he would have survived. Fighting was not in his skill set.

He changed into whatever clothes Bob handed him. As instructed, he gave his prison jumpsuit to Bob.

"The Captain's gonna wanna incinerate these," Bob told him. "Job time. Follow me."

Naria stared at her reflection after changing out of her prison uniform. Grabbing scissors in her one hand, her other hand pulled her long, raven hair away from her head. She held her breath as she snipped the first lock. Raven strands curled on the floor. After she placed the scissors down, she glanced at her handiwork. Her signature dark, long hair was now chopped close to her head. Her ears and neck felt exposed. With a snap of her fingers, a robot eliminated all the evidence of her previous hairdo.

When Naria returned to the bridge, Wretch stared at her. "Whadya do?"

"What needed to be done. Is it time?" asked Naria.

"Almost," said Wretch. "Ten seconds."

"Warm up the engines," Naria ordered.

"Engines warming," said Gorm.

The ship began to hum, then died to silence.

"What happened?" Naria asked.

Gorm frantically checked his screens. "I don't know. Bob, what's going on back there?"

Over the intercom, Bob said, "Nothing. Turbines won't spin."

The orange flashed brightly.

"Five seconds," said Wretch. "We need to get out of here or we'll be toast."

"Don't need to tell me," said Gorm. "Come on." His fingers pounded the panel feverishly.

Naria watched the nebula's lightning storm increase. "Puff the ship."

"We'll be hit for sure," Gorm protested.

"I'm counting on it," Naria said calmly.

"We'll fry," said Gorm.

"Or the lightning will give us the energy boost we need to leave this cloud," Naria countered.

"Two seconds," Wretched counted down.

"Do it," Naria barked.

Reluctantly, Gorm pressed the button. The sleek black ship's back end opened like a flower.

"One," said Wretch.

"Turn it on," said Naria.

Gorm turned the engines back on as a large strike hit the ship. The jolt almost knocked them out of their seats. Lights flickered. The engines hummed.

"Fly us out of here, Wretch," instructed Naria.

The orange gave way to expansive darkness.

"I can't bring the ship back in," said Gorm. "Need to go back and assess." He left the bridge.

"Where to, Captain?" Wretch asked.

"Pele."

Chapter 2

From the sanctuary of his penthouse atop Galaxy Tower, Kane gazed upon lush green gardens, which sat in the center of the precisely planned city of Galaxis. He grew more impatient with each passing second. Finally, the door slid open.

"Well?" he asked, without turning to face the entrant.

"Torquor Prison has been stabilized," said the man. "The dead have been identified."

"Is she one of them?" Kane asked, turning to stare at the messenger.

"No. She is not among the dead nor anywhere in the prison," he reported.

Kane placed his hands behind his back. His cool demeanor did not crack. "She must be found. I want her alive."

"Yes, Your Excellency," the messenger said while bowing.

Returning his attention to outside the window wall, he stared at the sky above the buildings. "Where are you, Naria? What have you done with it?"

"You are needed in Circle Chambers, Your Excellency," said a female voice. A redheaded android tidied his desk from his tea.

Kane tore himself away from the window. The hallway leading to Circle Chambers echoed with his footsteps. When the doors slid open, all he could see was MWG emblazoned on the floor. The M sat above the W as if they were mirror images of each other. The G both crossed and encircled the reflected letters. Glancing upwards, he found the other eight dignitaries already there.

Stepping on a small circle, the Equalift raised him to his spot among the dignitaries. The nine of them floated at equal levels in a circle in the middle of the large room. Only air separated them.

The dignitaries of the Milky Way Circle were equals in every way. All of them held the title of His or Her Excellency, except one. Every five years, the Circle voted among themselves a Conductor, who carries the title of His or Her Eminence.

"I gathered you all here to discuss the breach at Torquor Prison," said an austere woman. On the floor, the Milky Way Galaxy emblem glowed. A hologram of the prison floating in space appeared in the center of their circle. "The breach occurred in sector C-five." The hologram zoomed inside the prison to show the block of cells. "It then overflowed to sectors C-six, D-two, E-four, and F." Those sectors glowed. "Eighteen prisoners and five guards died." Faces of men and woman joined the prison hologram. "Dozens were injured. Six prisoners escaped." Six faces replaced the other holograms.

Kane only had eyes for one. Her long, raven hair framed dark eyes that pierced him. Contempt bubbled inside his cool exterior.

"If I may, Your Eminence," said another dignitary.

"Yes, Emmery?" Her Eminence allowed.

"Escapees are not our concern," said Emmery. "Let the Flyers do their job."

"If it were any other prison, then I would agree with you," Her Eminence countered. "Criminals cannot be incarcerated in Torquor Prison without our approval. The prison is touted as the most secure in the Galaxy. The deaths and injuries can look to be the result of some sort of accident. The escapes cannot. I am afraid the breach will not be able to be kept quiet for long. We need to have a plan to satiate the people and quell any fears.

"People have ingested everything we have fed them. We keep them safe from the dangerous parties because of that prison. They will demand more from us if they discover what we have told them may not be the entire truth."

Silence filled Circle Chambers. The state of the Galaxy Coalition could falter. Dignitaries of the Milky Way Circle were the beginning and the end. Only *they* knew what was best for the Milky Way. They were the reason people had food to eat, shelter, clothing, riches, security, peace of mind, and happiness. The nine of them approved everything that had to do with governing the people. Over a century's worth of work to unify almost all the planets and moons in the Milky Way under one governing body—the Milky Way Circle—could be undone by six derelicts or only one.

Chapter 3

The job was menial grunt work, but Lorne did not mind. No one on the ship trusted him. Trust was earned on a Pirate ship. Lorne, however, had to trust his shipmates. His fate was in their hands.

"Bob, get Pistol!" Gorm yelled as he ran past an unnoticed Lorne.

When he reached the machine room, Gorm stopped running. Staring at what did not move, he ran a hand through his thinning hair.

"What's up?" asked Pistol. She and Bob knew something was wrong.

"Won't condense. Need to rein it in manually," Gorm answered. "We shouldn't be seen heading to Pele."

"Where do you want us?" asked Bob.

Gorm sighed. "This is a four man job. Grab the new guy."

Walking into the hallway, Bob yelled, "Hey, New Guy!"

Lorne knew Bob meant him. Cautiously, he walked in the direction of Bob's voice.

Upon seeing Lorne, Bob said, "We need your help."

When they entered the machine room, Gorm said, "Bob and the new guy will take the far crank. Pistol, you're with me."

Lorne followed Bob. "What are we doing?" Lorne asked.

"The nebula storm must have fried the power to the expanders," explained Bob.

"Expanders?"

"This ship's an old blossom style cargo ship. Hardly see them around anymore. The back two-thirds open to increase storage space," Bob told him. "Of course, the Captain has modified. The titanium shell has been bonded with hematite—gives it the dark color that makes it hard to see and the magnetism confuses detection systems. Comes in real handy."

They arrived at a large metal pillar rising out from the floor. Bob pushed on the top of the pillar. Spokes protruded from its center to form a large wheel. Bob maneuvered his body between two of the long spokes.

"Across from me," Bob told Lorne. "Push when I say." He waited to see the light indicating that Gorm and Pistol were ready. When it turned steady yellow, he said, "Push."

The two men moved the spokes. After feeling slightly dizzy from going around, Lorne asked, "How do we know when to stop?"

"It'll tighten."

Lorne's arms tired from pushing. The spokes became harder to turn.

"Just a little more," said Bob.

Throwing his weight into the spoke, Lorne could no longer

feel his biceps. Or the pain in his arms and back overtook his body and everything felt the same. He could not be sure.

Bob saw the light turn green. "Stop. All locked down."

When Bob pushed the top of the pillar, the spokes retracted inside. "Why did we do that?" Lorne asked.

"The bud shape helps to get in and out of a planet's atmosphere easier," said Bob. He began walking away from the pillar. "You don't know much about ships."

Following, Lorne said, "No. They've only transported me from planet to planet. And even then, it was only once every few years or so."

Not being the curious type, Bob said nothing.

Lorne was glad that Bob did not inquire further. He missed his previous life, but he did not want to talk about it. He was content to keep his memories locked inside his head.

"Ship's condensed," Wretch announced. "Locking Pele's coordinates."

"Turn off the coms. I don't want to take chances of being discovered," ordered Naria.

No ship willingly went to Pele. The planet had no supplies, no inhabitants, no tourism, or any discernable value. Its inhospitable atmosphere murdered the lungs. Volcano ash spewed skyward every few minutes, making any trip dangerous. Sometimes dangerous became inevitable, especially in their line of work.

Naria left Wretch to pilot the Tigerlily alone. She traversed the metal corridors. Near the back of the ship, she found Bob with Lorne. Quickly glancing at the stowaway, she said to Bob,

"Get the drop ready. We're running as silently as possible. When in place, don't move."

Watching her walk away, Lorne could see authoritative strength emanating from her.

"Don't get any ideas," Bob said to him.

"Ideas?" he asked.

"The Captain is an attractive woman, but she'll sooner cut off your manhood if she gets a whiff of thoughts about her."

"I wasn't thinking like that," Lorne said. "Just want to do my work."

"Well, work's gonna have to wait until we're clear of Pele," Bob said.

Following him, Lorne asked, "Why?"

"No one's really allowed to go to Pele," Bob explained. "Too many ships crash on that forsaken planet. Volcanic ash is so fine that it can get into the ship's systems. Makes a real mess. No rescue ship will risk Pele. It's a death trip. Chance you take going there."

"Why are we taking that chance?" Lorne queried further.

"Pele's also the best place to dispose of incriminating items," said Bob. "Like your prison clothes and your trackers. Fewer things we have to worry about if we get searched. It's the same reason we flew into that nebula storm. Wipes out the ship's flight history. No one can prove we were anywhere near Torquor Prison."

"Won't it be in the computer that we went to Pele?"

"Going to Pele isn't illegal, just stupid. But, the computer is also buggy from being hit with nebula lightning," said Bob. "By the time Gorm fixes everything, it won't show we've been anywhere."

Bob grabbed the dirty beige bundle. Placing the bundle inside a metal claw, he ratcheted the claw closed.

"We're doing this manually," said Bob. "Stay here and do exactly what I say."

Glancing at his and Naria's prison uniforms securely in the claw, Lorne nodded.

Chapter 4

Kane paced across the stone floor of his office. Naria's defiant expression burned the back of his eyes.

"Transport is ready, Your Excellency," said the android.

A side door opened. Kane hurried through a long, glass-enclosed corridor. Doors glided open as he approached.

Under a glass dome, a transport pod waited. The metal hatch-like door softly opened towards the floor, revealing steps. After climbing the steps, the door locked tightly behind him.

Sitting in the front seat, he strapped the harness over his body. His hand gripped the stick yoke. With a touch of a button, the dome melted into the floor. He felt a slight vibration as the pod lifted off its platform.

The city's sparkling gray and glass skyscrapers did not interest Kane. He flew over bullet trains that zipped through the city. The gray sprawled for miles from the doughnut shaped center tower that housed the Milky Way Circle.

Finally seeing green fields, he checked his coordinates.

Fields ended with dense forest. The trees gave way to golden grasslands. He began his descent.

Kane landed on a flat rock surrounded by tall grass. Unlatching his harness, he stepped to the rear of the transport pod. At his touch, a panel disappeared. His hand grabbed the dark blue gun and two battery sticks. One stick, he tucked safely into his pocket. The other, he glided into the gun's handle until it clicked. Finger resting on the trigger, he opened the stepped door.

The grasses waved in the winds. He hated being outside the city. Wading through waist high grass was an unfortunate necessity. Finally, he found the rudimentary hut in the middle of nowhere. His knuckles rapped on the shabby piece of metal acting as a door.

"Who goes there?" asked a deep, raspy voice.

"I have an appointment," Kane answered.

The door opened. "Payment," demanded the man at the door.

Kane handed him the bag of tools and parts he was asked to bring as a consulting fee.

After checking the bag's contents, the man said, "Follow me."

Keeping a firm grip on his gun by his side, Kane followed the man down a long hall. The hut did not look to be as big from the outside. The man parted a curtain at the end of the hall. "He's waiting for you."

Kane passed through the curtain alone.

A haze surrounded the soft light. His nostrils detected a faint aroma of an illegal substance. At the back of the room, he saw a low cushioned seating area on which a man lounged.

"Are you going to shoot me?" the man asked.

Stashing the gun into his belt, Kane asked, "You are Dirk?"

"The one and only. Sit. What can I do for you?"

Kane sat on a low couch across from Dirk. Only an even lower table separated the men. "Something was stolen from me. I need you to find the thief."

Dirk let out a hearty laugh. "You have Flyers at your disposal for such a thing." He leaned back. "A member of the Circle wouldn't seek me for that kind of menial task."

"The thief is clever," Kane replied.

"Stole something of great importance. Perhaps something you hope others won't find." Dirk studied the man's shifting demeanor to get his answer. "Does this thief have a name?"

"A Pirate. Goes by the name of Naria."

Dirk blinked. "Captain Naria?" Leaning forward, he smiled. "She is ruthless, dangerous, and clever is an understatement. A perfect woman, really. She'll make it sporting. Do you want just her or her and whatever it was she stole?"

Kane searched Dirk for weakness. Examining his tattooed face and arms, he figured Dirk could handle a simple task. His reputation as a Bounty Hunter preceded him. "If she doesn't have it, then I need her alive. If she does, I'd prefer her dead."

Dirk did not think he heard correctly. He could not imagine a Galaxy where Naria did not roam. But, he could live in that Galaxy. "This is an expensive proposition."

"Name your price," said Kane.

Prices were always based on the client's position as well as the job. The man sitting across from Dirk held one of the nine highest positions in the Galaxy. Expecting to negotiate, Dirk started high. "I get paid half up front and half when I deliver." He popped open a hologram screen over the table between them. "Deposit seven million Ions into this account," the bank screen floated in front of them, "then I can start. After I retrieve the Captain, I want her ship, the Tigerlily, as final payment."

Staring at the blinking cursor, Kane said, "Deal." After transferring the funds, Kane gladly left the Bounty Hunter's hut. He quickly started the transport pod, then flew back to his landing pad in civilization.

Chapter 5

"Pele's in view, Captain," Wretch announced.

"No other ships for three quadrants," added Gorm.

Naria stared at the dark clouded planet. "Let's make this a quick in and out. Gorm, search for a lava pool."

The ship's computer scanned the planet's surface as the Tigerlily fell into orbit. "Found one," said Gorm.

"Entering atmosphere." Wretch changed the settings as the dark clouds grew closer. "Transitioning to Stone Mode." A light green grid covered the viewing window. The ship shuddered faintly.

"What was that?" Lorne asked Bob. They waited in the belly of the ship, wearing breathers over their faces.

"Pele has a thick atmosphere. Not every planet is as hard of an entry," Bob answered. He placed the cloth bundle on top of a hatch in the floor. Pointing, he said, "That lever beside you operates this first door. The lever behind you opens the door below it. Got that?"

Lorne nodded.

Rising, Bob placed his hands on a small, vertical wheel. "Get ready."

The sharp descent threw Lorne onto his back. Bob laughed. Righting himself, Lorne could feel the ship level.

"Open the first!" yelled Bob.

Using both hands, Lorne pulled the lever until it locked into position. "Open!" he yelled back.

Bob turned his wheel. The bundle dropped into the large cylindrical shaft. "Now close just until the doors touch the rope."

Lorne followed instructions. He watched Bob grab the claw's ratchet on the rope. "Open the second," Bob instructed. "It's going to get awfully windy in here."

Moving to the second lever, Lorne grasped tightly. As soon as the lever began to part the bottom doors, a warm wind howled into the ship's belly. He could smell the sulfur through his breather. Lorne was used to the creeping smells of dirt and gases that escaped from the depths of planets. The intense sulfur reeked as it clung to the metal. It had no escape. Sickness bubbled in his stomach. Trying to tune it out, he watched Bob ratchet the claw open.

Bob straddled the opening in the doors. The lava glowed below the crack in the doors. He peered at the claw as he ratcheted. Finally, the claw released the bundle. The red lava devoured the beige prison clothes and rice-sized trackers from both Naria and Lorne.

Jumping off the doors, Bob screamed over the wind's roar. "Open the first!"

Lorne pulled the first lever as Bob turned the wheel to raise the claw.

On the bridge, Naria stared at the white translucent smoke and blue rock formations. She wanted to scream over the coms and ask what was taking so long. Gorm's screen blinked orange. The bottom hatch was still open.

The wind forced Bob to raise the claw slowly. He did not want to damage the fire shield. The rope swayed violently. He listened for the scraping of metal.

The wind calmed. The rope stopped swaying. Bob turned the wheel quickly.

A warning beep echoed in the bridge. "Something's gonna blow," said Gorm.

"We need to move," said Wretch.

"Hatch still isn't closed," Gorm said.

Naira watched the grid covered window fill with white smoke. "Get ready, Wretch."

Believing he was clear of the bottom door, Bob screamed, "Close the second!"

Lorne pressed his weight onto the rear lever.

The light on Gorm's screen stopped blinking. "Go!" barked Naria.

Wretch steered the ship away from the lava. The serene lava pool exploded. Erupting gas knocked the Tigerlily through the sky.

Both Bob and Lorne rolled onto the just closed first door. "Guess she didn't like her offering," said Lorne.

"Or liked it too much," Bob countered. "I thought Wretch could fly."

"Wretch!" yelled Gorm.

Naria picked herself off the floor. Under the controls, Wretch did not move. A rapid beeping rang in Naria's ears. The Tigerlily quickly approached a large chunk of blue.

Leaping over the metal railing, Naria landed in front of the control panel. "We can't help her if we all die," she said. She placed her hand on the steering pad. The beeping subsided as she swerved, avoiding the mountain. White smoke began to cover the grid again.

"Ascend left," said Gorm.

The Tigerlily raced through the thick clouds. Piercing through Pele's volatile atmosphere, the black ship reached the calm of space.

"We need to check our damage," said Naria. "I'm setting co-ordinates for the Black Hole. Take Wretch to the infirmary."

Chapter 6

The gray ship was typical in every sense of the word. It had one, very large back hatch for loading and unloading and a small, but functional bridge. The captain's quarters were a decent size. The ship had served Dirk well. He thought it would do fine until he commandeered the Tigerlily.

He remembered the first time he stepped onto the Tigerlily. It was also the first time he had met Naria. At the time, he was foolish enough to believe that Gorm captained that spectacular ship. All his dealings had been with Gorm. Had he known he was collaborating with the Devil herself, he might not have taken the job.

The job ended well enough. His pockets burst with Ion filled stick tabs and he got to keep all his body parts. That was the last time he stepped onto the Tigerlily. After that one job, he admired the ship from afar. Every run-in with Naria was kept distant and cordial.

A part of him admired Naria while another part of him feared her. She was feared throughout the Galaxy. Just the mention of her name could send shivers down hardened criminals' spines. Fear equaled respect. If he were the one to take her down, then all that fear and respect would transfer to him. He smiled.

"Ship's loaded and ready to go," said the man with the deep, raspy voice.

"What about her crew?"

"Skeletal at best. Should we pick up a few of our regulars along the way?"

"Yes, but only regulars. This is a hunt best kept under wraps."

The man nodded.

"Make sure the shack's locked down, Cheat," Dirk told him. "This could be a long hunt."

Dirk walked up the ramp into the belly of his ship. He entered the bridge, then waited for Cheat to join him.

Cheat entered, saying, "All secure. Where to?"

"Doran. We'll take who we can from there," commanded Dirk. The motor's hum vibrated his feet. He spied the glistening gray city in the distance.

He never cared for the towering glass and steel monstrosities. Transport pods flittered from building to building. Those commuting vehicles could not reach more than a couple of hundred feet into the sky. He always had higher aspirations.

Breaking through the atmosphere, stars against black replaced the hazy curved horizon. "Engaging supers," Cheat announced.

The ship sped away from the planet. He looked out the glass into space. Without knowing exactly what Naria stole, he tried to predict her movements.

Unlike other Pirates and thieves in the galaxy, Naria did not sit in some space pub, boasting about her latest score. She sat in the corner, listening carefully. The boastful idiots had their scores stolen soon after. Some publicly accused the reclusive Naria.

Dirk recalled paying for information in a space pub when one of the unlucky accused her of stealing his horde in her presence. From her cloistered corner, her dark eyes shot into the room. The man pointed at her. She flicked a blade across the room. The sharp metal pinned the man's arm to the bar. Screams penetrated the pub. She slithered to the bar with a pen laser in her hand. "You want to say that again?"

The man screamed in pain.

"I didn't think so," she said. Pulling the blade out of his arm, she wiped his blood off on his shirt.

Dirk found himself smiling at the memory. Where would a woman such as she go? What would she need? And where would she get it?

"Flyers entering the quadrant," alerted Cheat.

Dirk groaned. "Prepare to be monitored and boarded," he said with disgust. "Transfer power in case they snare us. We don't need their lasers blowing the circuits."

He leaned back in his chair, watching the pink dots approach. *Schmact nuisance robots.* He longed for the days when law enforcement were red-blooded humans and easily bribable. The robot replacements annoyed him.

Robots patrolled every big city on every important planet in the Galaxy. All Interplanetary Transports had them. Any robot, anywhere, programmed to do anything, could be turned into a Patrolbot under Galaxy command.

Most ships supplemented their crews with robots for cleaning and maintaining the engines. Dirk was not so stupid. Every circuit board was Galaxy made and therefore Galaxy controlled. The Milky Way could monitor every move and listen to every word through the robots. He would rather not let the Galaxy know how he hunted his bounty. All he cared about was collecting his lons until he decided to retire.

"Flyers are requesting a dock," said Cheat.

The thought of police androids on his ship made his skin crawl. "Let's get this over with," Dirk responded. Disgusted, he trudged to the airlock to greet his unwanted guests.

Chapter 7

Gorm sat on a stool, watching Wretch lay on an infirmary bed. The three-dimensional hologram above her assessed the body scan.

"How is she?" Naria asked from the doorway.

Reading the report, Gorm said, "Knocked out. She may have a bump on her head. Hopefully, she'll wake up before we get to the Black Hole."

"Go make your shopping list," Naria said. "Tell Pistol and Bob to do the same. We'll meet in the Dine. Bring the stowaway."

Naria took Gorm's place on the stool. Wretch was the best pilot she had ever known. The Galaxy Corps' loss was the Tigerlily's gain. Sure, Naria knew how to fly her ship, but Wretch was a master. Wretch was a big part of her secret weapon against the Flyers. Only Wretch could out maneuver the Galaxy scum's laser snares.

"Did we crash?" asked Wretch, opening her eyes.

"Nope. Amazingly, I still remember how to fly," Naria said.

Wretch laughed weakly.

"Rest. We'll wake you when we get to the Black Hole."

As Wretch closed her eyes, Naria slipped out of the infirmary.

Lorne followed Bob to a door whose faded letters spelled D-I-N-E. "How old is this ship?" Lorne asked.

Bob laughed. "The Captain reclaimed it from a scrap planet." Two chairs slid out from under a long, metal table. "Been updated to be fwhee. All the robotics on board are Gorm's own designs. I even helped construct a few."

"Own design," Lorne repeated.

"Use all my own parts," Gorm said, approaching the table. "That way I know the Galaxy is not in them."

Lorne remembered his robot assistant. Sift journeyed with him to every planet. He gathered and analyzed. On the Interplanetary Transport, they finalized a report. Sift detained him moments before Flyers barged into their compartment. Cuffed, Lorne was thrown through an airlock into a cell. During his "trial," he discovered why he was snatched from his life. His robot betrayed him, but it was not really *his* anyway.

"What do we have?" Naria asked, entering with Pistol.

"An expensive parts list," said Gorm.

"And we're out of nitrobooster," Pistol added. "If we're doing the run I'm thinking, we're going to need it."

"We also need Wretch," said Gorm.

Naria's dark eyes rested on Gorm. "How long will it take to repair the ship?"

"If we can do it while docked in the Black Hole, a couple of hours," Gorm answered. "And everyone helps. If I have to spacewalk, I don't know."

"Can you start without everything on your list?"

"Yes, but who's going to see Trick?"

She studied her crew. Gorm, Bob and Pistol could fix the ship. Her eyes found Lorne. She knew nothing about him. His light eyes gave him away. "You're analytical," she said. "Used to delicate work. You're out of your element, but its time you earned your keep."

Lorne swallowed.

"The Circle won't admit that Torquor Prison was breached," continued Naria. "No one is going to know your face."

"He needs a new name," said Pistol.

After a moment, Naria said, "Rock."

Lorne smiled to himself.

"Don't flatter yourself," she said. "It's not meant in *that* way."

His smile melted. "Tha... that's not ha... how I took it," he stammered. "I'm a geologist. Or, I was. Once."

A wicked smile spread across her face. "Really? Useful." Naria's dark gaze lingered longer than he would have liked. "Give him the list and fit him with some weapons."

Wanting to protest, Lorne sat as Gorm and Pistol swooped upon him. Gorm handed him a piece of mesh, saying, "These are listed in order of importance. Get as much as you can with what we have to trade."

"Come, Rock," said Pistol. "I'm going to make you look as schmact as your name." She led him through a door disguised as a wall.

The room was bigger than he thought it could be. Crates crowded the center of the room. Walking around them, he stared at the different sized weapons adorning the walls.

"Amazing, right?" she said, smiling. "I've procured some great and unique weapons over the years. You are getting a photon rifle and...." She strolled around the room. Stopping, she picked up, "...an old-fashioned revolver. The chamber holds six bullets, but with this baby, you only need one." She tenderly caressed the hunk of metal. "Also, I don't allow anyone to leave the ship without a pen laser. It will cut through everything. Eventually."

"But I don't know how to use any of this stuff," said Lorne.

Pistol laughed. "You're not going to need to. It's all for show. The Black Hole is an out of the way, hidden space hub. Not to mention, well out of the Flyers' reach. We can supply safely there. It's the best place in the Milky Way for black market goods. Personally, I prefer the Flower Bazaar on Daisy. They have some of the best weapons I didn't steal myself."

Lorne returned to his modest quarters to study the list. "I don't belong here," he muttered. Being on the Pirate ship was better than prison. He knew that he could never return to his old life. He had to fashion a new life. Did he have to leave Lorne behind and become Rock to do so? His heart skipped a beat.

Chapter 8

The news of the prison explosion tore through the Galaxy. Memorials to the prison guards were erected around Galaxis. People laid flowers and small globe lights next to the pictures of those who had passed in the accident.

The Circle spun the breakout as an energy overload from wandering stardust radiation. Kane did not visit the memorials in person. He and the other Circle dignitaries appeared as holograms to console the mourning. Of course, the people clamored for the Milky Way Galaxy to do something to protect innocent lives from rogue stardust. The Circle assured the people that they would do everything in their power to keep Milky Way citizens safe.

Patrolbots captured two of the six escapees. The remaining four's pictures had been circulated to every Flyer in the Milky Way. None of the surveillance scanned any of Naria's facial or body features. It was only a matter of time, as far as Kane was concerned. His hired Bounty Hunter was simply extra insurance.

"Your Excellency," said a female voice. "Flyers have rendezvoused with the Bounty Hunter. He seems to be holding up his end of the bargain." A longhaired redhead stood next to his desk in a flowery lace gown. "Your tea is being prepared. Are you ready for your massage?"

He studied the lace. Bare manufactured skin peeked through the loops. His personal assistant catered to his every need. Her skin, her hair, her personality—none of it was real, but he did not care. Wanting to peek behind the lace shroud, he said, "Set up the table. I'll be right there."

Kane focused his fleeting attention on the dot indicating Dirk's ship. The Bounty Hunter headed towards an insignificant planet. He did not care why, as long as it led to Dirk retrieving his stolen property.

Shutting off the hologram, he rose from his desk. His redheaded android held a steaming cup of herbal tea next to a massage table. He sipped, knowing that he would not be able to fully relax until what Naria stole was back in his possession. While the redhead undressed him, he figured he could try.

Chapter 9

Bars and scorpions littered the dusty streets of New Arizona. Dirk passed the General Store without a peek through the grit-laden windows. New Arizona was a well-worn city, although no one would admit to ever being there. It did not have the glitz or glamor of Galaxis. No fancy boutiques lined its unpaved avenues. People traveled there to get away from the prying eyes of the Patrolbots and savor more unsavory delights.

A battered wooden sign swung over Dirk's head. Reading, "Fox and Hound," he entered. An older woman greeted him from behind a desk in a cozy, sterile lobby. "May I help you?" she asked with a smile.

"I have an appointment with two-two-three," Dirk said.

The woman pressed a button. A young teenage boy entered through a door behind her. After she whispered in his ear, he nodded.

"Follow me," the boy said. They climbed a narrow staircase. A few men and a couple of women exited rooms off a long hallway.

The boy unlocked a door with a metal key. Opening the door, the boy recited his spiel. "We're a clean facility, so please use the cleansing station. Anti-transfer spray is provided. Your Eroi will be right with you. Tips are always welcome. Pay at the front desk when you leave." He closed the door behind Dirk.

In the center of the room, he waited. Dirk would not sit on any of the chairs and consciously avoided the bed.

A man entered through a door on the opposite end of the room, wearing nothing more than a sock below his rippling abs. "Oh, it's you," he said.

"Don't sound so disappointed, Drake," said Dirk.

"I was hoping you'd be a real customer," Drake said, flopping on the bed.

Dirk dropped a bag of spare parts on the table. "I'll make this quick. What do you know about a Pirate named Naria?"

Raising his eyebrows, Drake said, "Take your scraps and go."

"You're loyal to her? What is she, one of your regulars?"

"It's not like that," Drake said. "You saved my life, Dirk. My loyalty lies with you. I just don't have anything to tell you about her."

"What about her crew? Pistol? Gorm? Wretch? Bob?"

Sighing, Drake propped himself on his elbow. "I may have seen Pistol browsing the Flower Bazaar on Daisy not too long ago. Bought untraceable explosives. She said that she was experimenting, but she bought much more than for experiments."

Perhaps to break someone out of a highly secure prison, Dirk thought.

"You want info about Naria, go see my former employer."

"Trick?"

Drake nodded. "Be prepared to pay gobs of lons. Don't mention me. That's *if* you can find him."

"Thanks." Dirk left the bag on the table as he walked out.

When he reached the bottom of the stairs, a woman wearing a satin corset under a see-through robe stood in a doorway. "A word," she said.

He entered her boudoir without question.

"Sit," she ordered.

Carefully, he sat on a red, poufy chair.

Lounging on a chaise, she took a long drag from a pipe. "I let you come and go as you please, Dirk," she stated. "Drake, who you found for me, is an excellent employee. He brings in the lons. Women love him and some men. For years, I have tolerated your fact-finding missions in my establishment. It's time I cashed in the favor you owe me."

Dirk waited for her to continue while she puffed on her pipe.

"Being an Eroi is not for everyone," she lectured. "That's why the oldest profession is overrun with androids. There is still something to be said for the human connection. That is why people seek us. Anyway, I need you to take a girl off my hands."

"A girl, Madam?"

"Take her anywhere she wants to go, within reason."

"It's not a good time. I'm hunting a dangerous criminal."

She laughed. "You're always chasing someone or something."

"Who is going to look after this girl?" Dirk asked.

"She can look after herself." Getting up, she pressed a button near the door.

A figure of a woman entered the room. Dirk noticed her large travel bag.

"Selina," said Madam, "this is the man I mentioned, Dirk."

Dirk's eyes traveled up from her boots, over her clothes, which could never hide a weapon, to her face. Selina was barely a woman.

"You're welcome back here anytime," Madam told Selina.

Selina half smiled. "Thanks."

Madam made a weak attempt to hug her, but did not.

"Good-bye," Selina said, then walked out the other door with her bag.

"Take good care of her," Madam said to Dirk.

Selina and her bag waited in the lobby. She followed Dirk onto the dusty streets.

"I don't run a shuttle service," Dirk told her.

"I know what you do," Selina replied.

He led her into one of the bars. "Madam told you?"

"She told me enough," she said. They sat at a table in the back corner of the room. "I am not a child."

"Never said you were."

A waitress brought drinks while Dirk studied the room. No one batted an eyelash at Dirk sitting with such a young woman. That was what he liked about Doran. People minded their own business. When Cheat entered, he immediately walked to their usual table.

Sitting with them, Cheat stared at Selina.

"Cheat is my First Mate and pilot," he said. "Selina will be joining us."

"We got everything we needed," Cheat mentioned without taking his eyes off of her.

Dirk caught a glimpse of Selina's plump lips caressing the rim of her glass. As she downed her drink, he knew that bringing her aboard his ship was a bad idea. Hoping that he would be dropping her off at the next stop, he said, "Let's get off this poorly terraformed rock."

Once inside the ship, the crew stared at her. She either did not notice or did not care. Following Dirk and Cheat to her room, she studied the interior. They stopped at her door.

"It isn't much, but it'll do," said Dirk.

She smiled. "I'm sorry you got roped into my mother's idea of a lifetime of reparations for choosing whoring over her daughter." Taking her bag from Cheat, she entered the room, closing the door behind her.

Her mother? Dirk shook his head. "Take her to black, Cheat. We need to find the Black Hole."

Chapter 10

"Docking permission for the Black Hole has been granted," said Gorm. "They'll be beaming us in as soon as we are in range."

"Good. We need the rest," replied Naria.

"Do you think it's a good idea to let the new guy negotiate for our supplies alone?" Gorm asked.

"Trick knows us. Do you have a better idea?" Naria stared into the eternal spotted darkness from the pilot's chair.

"Actually," he said quietly, "I've been working on something."

The Black Hole's homing beam took control of the ship. "Have Bob dock her," she said.

Leaving the bridge, she walked down the metal corridor. Her knuckles rapped on a metal door. The door opened. "Rock, it's time," she said.

Lorne took a deep breath, then followed her through the ship.

"Trick is a brutal man, but fair," Naria explained. "He

measures a man by how he presents himself. The harder you look, the more he'll think you're his equal. And he'll treat you as such. Expect to be scanned for trackers and weapons. You won't be disarmed, he just likes to know. This isn't intragalactic net shopping. He's going to expect you to haggle. He likes the game, but don't push him too far. Oh, and if he asks you to do him a favor, don't—under any circumstances. You may want to keep all your body parts attached."

Gulping, Lorne did not understand why they had to resort to violence. They stopped near the airlock where Pistol waited.

"Arms out," Pistol said to Lorne. He obeyed. She garnished his body with weapons and ammo. Dripping in arms, he felt dirty. Lastly, she thrust a small cylinder in his hand. "Pen laser," she said. "Clasp your hand around it. Use your thumb to hit the on and off on the end." She wrapped a beige scarf around his neck and head. "He's ready."

"Docking in ten," Bob's voice announced.

"Heard," Naria replied.

Gorm clomped down the corridor towards them. When he reached Naria, he opened his hand. Three dots rested in his palm. "Three point hologram. Untraceable and undetectable."

Smiling, Pistol handed Naria weapons. "None of your usual," she said.

After wrapping her head in a matching scarf, Gorm attached the points. Her dark hair turned blonde and swept her jawbone. Sapphires replaced her dark eyes. Her complexion lightened so much that Pistol gave her gloves.

Gorm held up a mirror. "Schmact," Naria said. Her lips did not move.

"I'm still working out the bugs, but at least you won't look like you," he said. "Don't forget your coms." He gave each an ear bud. "Trick scrambles coms, so they'll be dead while you're in with him," he said to Lorne. "You got the list?"

"Yes."

He handed Lorne a stick tab. "Lons available for trade," Gorm said.

The Tigerlily clamped into its bay. An accordion terminal reached the airlock. Gorm hit the red "lock" on the pad near the door. It blinked until it said, "Ready," in green.

Releasing the pressurized doors, Gorm said, "Good luck."

Chapter 11

On the bridge, Dirk stared at the empty space quadrant hologram. "Are you sure the code's right?"

"Yes, but I think they've moved," Cheat answered.

"How does anyone find him if he keeps moving?" Dirk asked. He recalled his first trip to the Black Hole. Ironically, he was aboard the Tigerlily. He happened to be on the bridge when Gorm transmitted the code. "Read the code back to me."

"Bravo echo four seven lima romeo zero x-ray," Cheat stated.

"X marks the spot," Dirk muttered, remembering Gorm's words from years ago. He looked at Cheat. "X is the confirmation," Dirk said.

"Stop at zero?" Cheat asked. "Doesn't make sense."

It did not make sense. Dirk pressed his fingers into his eyebrows. "Not zero," he said. "Theta. When printed, it looks like a zero."

"Theta? Where I am going to find that?"

"Earth archives," Dirk replied. "It's a letter from an ancient, dead, Earth language."

Cheat's stubby fingers grazed the control pad. "Found it." He mumbled, "Bravo echo four seven lima romeo theta." A dot appeared in the hologram. "They're asking for confirmation."

"X-ray," said Dirk.

Cheat smiled. "We've got coordinates. They'll beam us in once we reach it. How'd you know?"

"Sometimes, my former life comes in handy," Dirk mentioned.

"So, you weren't always a Bounty Hunter?" said Selina. "Sorry, I was looking for the galley."

Standing, Dirk said, "I'll show you where everything is." He ushered her into the corridor. "I used to be in antiques and relics. Bounty Hunting pays better."

"I would think that people would pay a universe of lons for an Earth relic," Selina said.

"They do," Dirk agreed. "Anything that is still around from Earth is rare and needs to be authenticated."

"Why not just go to Earth and harvest relics?"

"Some people do, if they're willing to risk the radiation levels. However, those don't fetch many lons. True relics have a history," Dirk explained. "A history that can't be faked, mind you. It's the history that makes the relic valuable. But unless you are the owner of the relic, there isn't much money in it. The commissions were decent enough. Brokerage license fees and android upkeep and associated fees ate most of your lons. I used my first finding fee as a Bounty Hunter to buy this ship. Haven't looked back since."

They entered the gleaming gray galley. Selina opened the cabinets, peeking inside each one. "So," said Dirk, "where is it that you want to go?"

Pausing her exploration, she leaned against the counter. "I spent the majority of my life in the mining community, RM three seven gamma. I didn't know much about life beyond. My dad recently died in a mining accident. That's how I came to be with my mother."

"I'm sorry about your father."

She smiled briefly. "Thanks. I feel adrift—like space junk." She stared at her feet. "I'll figure it out."

He left her searching in the galley. In the corridor, a tall, burly man caught up to him. "Scythe, is everything ready for our excursion?" Dirk asked.

"Yes," Scythe replied.

"Good. Cheat will be keeping the engines warm."

"Captain," said Scythe. "May I speak to you about something?"

Dirk waited.

Scythe checked the corridor, then said quietly, "Having that girl on the ship...." He paused. "She's... It's a bad idea."

He knew how Scythe felt. "She'll be gone soon enough." Knowing that he gave no real relief, he proceeded to his quarters.

With the door locked behind him, he pressed his palm into the underside of his desk. A compartment slid open. He grabbed two stick tabs from the small drawer. Each contained the maximum amount of lons—five hundred thousand. Placing them in an inner pocket, he hoped one million lons would suffice. "They'd have to," he mumbled. "No one is worth that much—not even her."

Chapter 12

Traipsing through the Black Hole, Lorne tried not to look around too much. He wanted to blend in as best he could. Everything in the space hub Lorne had seen in a museum. He found it hard not to peek at the old-styled architecture. Occasionally, they passed a panel or a door that was obviously much newer.

The amount of people conducting business in a criminals' hideout surprised him. He had no idea there were so many who lived on the other side of the law wandering the Milky Way. They traded everything—weapons, drugs, clothing, robotics, food, and items Lorne did not know. Vendors sold all that a person would need to survive and then some. Each vendor worked in a room-like stall. Customers either bartered with other items or the usual Ion filled stick tabs. He wondered how the Black Hole could operate on such a large scale without the Galaxy's knowledge.

Lorne followed the flaxen Naria who navigated the vintage hub with ease. The people with whom they walked wore hardened expressions. They entered an elevator where weapons adorned the packed bodies. People entered and exited the steel box at all different levels. Lorne peeked at firing ranges, bars, cafes, and lodging pods. Perhaps not all who patronized the Black Hole were criminals.

Naria finally nudged him through the elevator doors. He let her guide them through a maze of metal corridors.

A line formed in front of a panel over which flashed, *check-in*. Joining the queue, they did not wait long. Naria entered *Rock plus one* and *Tigerlily* at the prompts. They found seats in a small waiting area.

A step-in, whole body scanner separated them from Trick. It reminded Lorne of the ones at every spaceport. Lacking non-anthropomorphic robots, he wondered who tended the scanner. Names scrolled above its entrance. One by one, the waiting stepped inside. A wide beam of light wiped from head to toe. A door opened, granting the scanned person access. When the scanner beeped, denying further entry, armed men escorted the person down a corridor.

Lorne practically sprang off his seat when *Rock* scrolled. His heart beat faster as he entered the scanner. After a few seconds, the door on the other side opened. He held his breath, waiting for Naria. When the door slid into the side, she joined him.

Each step down the dim, narrow hallway felt more ominous. Lorne had no idea what he was doing. He purposefully chose a profession where he did not need to deal with people. Analyzing core samples was his strong suit. Robots and rocks on desolate planets gave him comfort. A door automatically opened. He needed to feel comfortable with whom he was supposed to be. If he made a mistake, either Trick or Naria could kill him.

Heavily armed men guarded the smooth walls of the virtually vacant room. Across from the door, a man sat on a chair like it was his throne.

"You must be Rock from the Tigerlily," the man said. His voice reeked of disbelief.

Yes, I am, thought Lorne. *I am Rock.* He took a quick breath through his nose. "And you are Trick?" Lorne asked in defiance.

"The one and only," answered Trick. "Tell me, how's Naria?"

He's testing, Naria thought. Trick would have known that she was sent to Torquor. She hoped Lorne would pass.

"How should I know?" Lorne quipped.

Trick's lips pursed. "Why did they send *you* to me? Why isn't Wretch here?" He glanced at the silent Naria.

Don't engage, Naria wished she could tell Lorne.

"I'm not here to chat, Trick. I'm here to trade. If you don't want our lons," said Lorne.

The right side of his mouth curled into a smirk. "Business man. Let's trade."

Lorne unrolled the mesh. With a twist of the electronic fabric, the list of items popped between him and Trick. Glaring through the hologram, he asked, "How much for everything on the list?"

Naria hated having to keep quiet. She wanted to scream, to take over the haggle. Laying it all out there for him to see was not her style. Lorne needed to threaten Trick more.

Trick's index finger stroked the patch of hair below his lower lip. Finally, he said, "Two twenty-five."

Gorm had warned Lorne about how Trick will use low numbers when he really meant two hundred twenty-five thousand lons. The stick tab in Lorne's pocket only contained one hundred seventy thousand lons.

Naria's heart raced. She hoped the holographic disguise hid the beads of sweat forming near her brow.

"One fifty," said Lorne.

"One hundred fifty thousand? Are you trying to insult me?" Trick rose off his throne.

"What would you give for one fifty?"

Sneering, Trick said, "A pack of nitroboosters, a box of converters, and an ionizer. However, I'll throw in everything else on the list, *if* you also do me a little favor."

"Please say no," Naria repeated in her head.

"How about for one fifty, I get two packs of nitroboosters, a spool of wire, and an ionizer. No favors," Lorne countered.

"You drive a hard bargain, Rock." Trick laughed. "I'll give you the box of converters, too. Give Wretch my best." He nodded sharply to one of his men.

The man opened a panel of wall. A robot rolled into the room with two boxes, then placed them on the floor. After inspecting the boxes' contents, Naria gave Lorne a nod.

Lorne entered one hundred fifty thousand on the stick tab. Touching his stick tab to Trick's stick tab, he pressed transfer. Both he and Naria carried the boxes out of Trick's trading room. While waiting for the elevator, Lorne's body relaxed, relieved that it was over.

The elevator lights indicating which level slowly changed. All Dirk wanted was to get in and out of the junk heap of a space hub as quickly as possible. He hated giving Naria so much space between them. Knowing her, she could be anywhere. He hoped that he would spot her amongst the sea of criminals crawling on every level. That sort of luck would not be his. Finally, the elevator brought him and Scythe to Trick's level.

Naria glimpsed a tattooed face exiting the elevator. He looked familiar, but she could not place him. Standing in the steel box, she watched the tattooed man strut down the corridor to see Trick. As they descended, her mind turned, trying to determine from where she knew the man.

Her brain removed the tattoos. She saw facial features that she recognized. He had spent time on her ship. "Schmact," she said under her breath. The elevator doors opened to their space dock level. Frantically weaving through the crowd, Naria covered her mouth with a box. "Warm up the engines. We're leaving as soon as we board," she said over the coms.

Bob waited at the airlock for Naria and Lorne. She pushed her boxes into Bob's hands. Extracting a small, metal cylinder from the top box, she said, "Get the boxes and yourselves secure. We leave now."

Not understanding the problem, Lorne followed Bob at a brisk pace.

Naria sprinted through the ship. "Undock! Undock!" she screamed over the coms. Entering the bridge, she glimpsed at Gorm and Wretch at their stations. "Dirk's here. I think he's hunting me."

The Tigerlily rose from its dock. At idle speed, Wretch flew with the flow of traffic leaving the Black Hole.

Chapter 13

At Trick's sign-in panel, Dirk entered *Scythe, plus one,* and *Tigerlily.* He would not dare type his own name for fear of getting rejected. Entering Tigerlily for the ship would get Trick's attention.

Dirk scanned the faces of everyone waiting to see Trick. No one looked remotely like Naria or her crew. Finally, Scythe's name scrolled above the scanner. Dirk waited his turn for the full body scan. After the green light passed over his body, he stepped out to meet Scythe.

When they entered Trick's spartan room, Trick demanded, "Who are you?"

"The name is Dirk."

"Get off my space hub before I force you off," Trick said. The armed men pointed their guns at Dirk and Scythe.

"I'll go, but don't you want to know why I'm here?"

Trick's teeth clenched. "I don't like being deceived." A door opened to the hall.

Dirk did not move. "You wouldn't have seen me otherwise. I'm willing to pay well for information," he said.

"What kind of information?" Trick leaned forward in his seat.

"I'm looking for Naria."

Chuckling, Trick dismissed Dirk. "Naria is in Torquor Prison."

"I have it on good authority that she's not," said Dirk.

"Who's authority?"

"*Excellent* authority."

The door to the hall closed. Trick studied the man with the tattooed face. He had heard of the Bounty Hunter, but had never met him. Many of his business associates received a one-way ticket to prison because of Dirk. Disposing of him while aboard his establishment would be easy. However, if Dirk had dealings with one of the Galaxy Circle, then doing so would be unwise.

"You have money?" Trick asked.

Dirk raised a stick tab. "Maxed."

"I can't tell you where Naria is."

"I just want some background information," said Dirk.

Resting on the arm of his chair, Trick began, "I haven't actually seen Naria for years. That's not to say she doesn't frequent the Black Hole. She just doesn't come to me. I prefer to deal with others on her crew. Naria sometimes will do business with the vendors or another person from time to time.

"From what I know of her, she commands a tight ship. Her crew is loyal. People fear her and her crew for good reason. Under all her strengths, and there are many, she has one weakness—precious stones and metals. She actively seeks outs dealers, stone cutters and metal workers."

Trick paused. "Now, I don't like giving up my customers, but I have one more piece of information—very valuable information. I'll tell you, if you agree to give me the entire contents of that stick tab."

Five hundred thousand lons was a lot of money. Dirk needed the information. If he believed that the info was not worth it, Dirk could not give him less. Trick's men would make living very unpleasant for both he and Scythe, if allowed to live. "It's a deal," Dirk told him.

"Naria has a place on a planet her ship has never gone," Trick said. "That place will never show on her ship's logs. Not that the Tigerlily is registered with the Galaxy, but one can find travel logs if one knows where to look. I highly doubt her crew has ever been there. She's clever enough to never have mentioned where, but I know her little refuge exists." Rising from his seat, he touched his stick tab to Dirk's. Five hundred thousand lons transferred. "It was a pleasure doing business. Now, I never want to see you again in my space hub."

A door opened. Dirk and Scythe walked down the corridor to the elevator a half million lons lighter.

Trick stored the full stick tab in a hidden compartment in his chair. "Flyers entering the quadrant," said a voice over the coms.

"Initiate emergency sequence," Trick stated. "Put us on lockdown." His hand swiped a panel on the wall. He entered a code, then waited for his retina scan.

The panel replied, "Purge all records?"

Trick touched *yes*. Once he read, "Purging all data," he and his men walked through a door to the Black Hole Command Center.

An alarm wailed throughout the space hub. People ran frantically through the corridors. Shops' inventories disappeared into the floor and walls. Calmly, Dirk and Scythe returned to the space dock.

Chapter 14

"The Black Hole sounded the alarm," Gorm announced. "Flyers. They're closing the exits to spin to a new location."

"Fly us out of here, Wretch," Naria ordered.

"We're not close enough," said Wretch.

Naria tossed the cylinder to Wretch. "We got two packs. I don't care where we go as long as it's far from here."

Lifting a small door on the console, Wretch pushed the cylinder inside. "Nitroboosting in eight," she said.

Bob locked the cargo door. "Seven," Wretch's voice counted down.

"Hurry," he told Lorne, "we need to get strapped in."

"Six."

Following Bob through the ship, Lorne listened to Wretch. "Five." They found Pistol already harnessed into a seat against the wall. "Four." Lorne slammed into a hard seat. "Three." Bob's straps clicked into place. "Two." Lorne pulled the harness across his chest. "One." *Click.* "Engaged."

The ship's force pressed them against their seats.

"Ship starboard," Gorm said.

Naria gripped the arms of her chair as she watched the space hub whiz past.

"Down," said Gorm.

"I can see," Wretch snapped.

"Doors closing. Fifteen meters," said Gorm. "Ten meters."

"Hold on," said Wretch. Her hands raced across the control pad.

The Black Hole's massive metal doors blocked the lessening view of space. Naria spied the interlocking teeth, hoping they would not be chomped.

The Tigerlily spun towards the closing teeth. Naria no longer felt her insides. The lights of the space dock disappeared.

"Out," Gorm announced. "Whoa. Swarms of Flyers."

"Magnetize," barked Naria.

"Magnetizing," Gorm repeated.

The glowing pink of Flyers filled the black.

"No! No! No! No! No! No!" yelled Gorm. He banged on the panel in front of him. "Magnetic generator down. Someone back there fix it!"

Gorm's angry frustration boomed over the coms. Unlatching his harness, Bob ran. Pistol and Lorne followed. The rocking ship slammed them into the metal walls and railings.

"If we keep this up, we're going to lose our gravity, too," said Bob.

"They're firing snares," said Gorm.

"I know," Wretch said through clenched teeth. She leaned

with the ship as she flew between the lasers.

Bob unscrewed a section of wall. A small closet held a floor to ceiling opened tube. Surrounding the tube, metal nodes sat a few inches away from what resembled a core sample drill to Lorne.

"I take it that thing is supposed to turn," said Lorne.

"It generates a magnetic field that blocks a Flyer's laser snare," Pistol explained. She handed Bob a testing tool.

"There's power, but I don't know why it won't spin," said Bob.

To analyze alien planet soil composition for terraforming, Lorne used drills that, more often than not, malfunctioned. "If there's a panel on the top, open it," he said. As Bob unscrewed, Lorne continued, "The purple and greens shouldn't be touching. Sometimes, the vibrations from rotation make them slip."

"Found them. They are touching," Bob said. He used two rods to separate the wires.

The drill spun rapidly. The nodes created a glow around the core. "Let's close this up," said Bob.

"Magnetic generator is running," said Gorm. He watched his screen. "We can repel snares ... now!"

The Tigerlily slipped smoothly between the Flyers.

"They don't even see us," said Gorm.

"Where to, Captain?" Wretch asked.

"We're going somewhere quiet and out of the way. We have repairs to finish," replied Naria. "But for now, let's just get past these Galaxy scum."

Chapter 15

Looking at the pink dots filling the hologram, Trick muttered, "Schmact." How did so many Flyers descend upon his space hub? "Karra! What's our status?"

"We're almost at full rotation speed, but they're sending snares," Karra reported.

He turned to one of his men. "Get me Dirk."

"Sir, the snares are slowing us down," Karra said. "We can't shake them without full rotation."

"Divert all power to the rotator," Trick ordered.

The lights on every level darkened. The elevator stopped. Its doors opened at the nearest level. Dim orange lights outlined the floors and walls.

Dirk and Scythe followed the emergency lights back to the ship. "Everything's on lockdown," said Cheat. "We're stuck here."

Strolling through his ship, Dirk mulled over Trick's words. He knew that he could never touch the Tigerlily's logs unless he was physically on the ship. Gorm had disabled the ship's data communication system. Data could not transfer in or out of the ship. He was unsure how he would find her refuge. In his experience, people always tended to go to wherever they considered home.

A loud banging echoed through the ship. Trick's men knocked on the airlock. Dirk had Scythe let them in. "Come with us. Trick wants to see you," one of the men said.

Having no choice, Dirk allowed the men to escort him through the dark space hub and up a pulley service elevator.

Dirk entered Trick's Command with his escorts. Seeing all the pink dots, he knew exactly why he was summoned.

"What did you do?" Trick asked through gritted teeth.

"They had to have tagged my ship. We did a sweep."

Trick stood inches from Dirk's face. "Not good enough!" He snapped his fingers, then pointed. Someone raced out of the room.

Beyond Trick, Dirk could see the pink dots moving into formation. "They're going to destroy you—the Black Hole and everything and everyone inside," Dirk warned.

"Sir, they're requesting docking privileges," Karra said.

"I don't want those robot schmact in my hub," barked Trick. He pushed a finger into Dirk's chest. "Get them to leave."

Turning to Karra, Dirk said, "Put them on coms."

"On," said Karra.

"This is Captain Dirk. We rendezvoused in sector bravo dash two."

"Captain Dirk," said a generic robotic voice. "We are initiating top sequence four two nine six four three zulu." The pink dots moved to another formation. "Have you found your bounty?"

"No. My bounty is not here."

"Can we offer assistance?"

He knew how he could find Naria. "Yes, but not here. Once my ship is permitted to leave, I would like permission to search flight logs."

"A Flyer will be waiting in this sector. Use communication code, lima two four tango."

"Thank you," said Dirk.

The pink dots scattered, except one.

"Get out," Trick ordered.

Chapter 16

Dirk practically sprinted through the space hub. The hub's normal lights sprang to life as he entered the docking bay. Boarding his ship, he announced over the coms, "We have permission to leave. Let's go before he changes his mind."

"Undocking," said Cheat's voice.

Scythe met Dirk in the corridor. "Trick's man found trackers aboard. They've been destroyed."

"Good. I'm tired of being followed." Dirk entered the bridge.

The chomping metal doors opened just enough for Dirk's ship to escape the Black Hole. Cheat navigated towards the waiting Flyer. Finally reaching full rotation, the Black Hole disappeared.

Dirk's ship docked with the Flyer. Only Dirk was permitted aboard.

The sleek Galaxy ship had no panels a human could access. A soulless humanoid met him on the flight deck. "Which flight logs?" it asked.

"Interplanetary Transport. Run a facial recognition search for Naria," Dirk requested.

"Running." After a few seconds, it said, "Found her. She was apprehended on Transport from Jullian to Congoland."

"And before Jullian?"

"Running partial recognition," the robot said. "She may have entered Jullian's spaceport from Laket, Toondah, Crepsil, or Atlas."

Dirk smirked at Naria's cunning. However, foxes always left footprints. "Follow the partial trails back in time. Then search for repeating patterns."

"Searching." After a long minute, the robot stated, "Trails end: Wakefield, Lumina, Pothos, Crank, and Turnsdale."

"Thank you."

"Do you need further assistance?"

"Not at the moment," said Dirk. "I need to gather more clues. I will let you know."

"Use the same communication code."

Once Dirk returned to his ship, the Flyer detached. "Pull a Trick," he said quietly to Scythe. With a nod, Scythe disappeared.

"Where to?" Cheat asked as Dirk entered the bridge.

Sitting in his chair, Dirk replied, "I'm thinking."

Cheat just stared at him until Scythe entered the bridge, saying, "Super clean."

"Bring up: Wakefield, Lumina, Pothos, Crank, and Turnsdale,"

Dirk ordered. "Which of those have something habitable within junket distance?"

With a few keystrokes, Cheat had the five planets on the screen. "Pothos has four moons, two are terraformed," said Cheat. "Crank has nothing a junket could reach. Neither does Wakefield. Turnsdale is the main planet of the Xenon planet cluster. Lumina is near a couple of junk planets—looks like terraforming didn't take."

Dirk studied the planets on the screen. "Lumina it is."

Chapter 17

Hearing grievances made the title of Excellency boring. However, the perks far outweighed the tiny time dealing with the people. The dignitaries of Galaxy Circle had to throw the people they governed something, lest they revolt. Not just anyone could live as a dignitary.

Kane accessed everything he would ever want in life. His penthouse overlooking Galaxis sufficed. His robot servants catered to his every need. He ate the best food and wore the best clothes the Milky Way offered. Superior medicines and other products and procedures gave him the health to outlive the people. The dignitaries had to remain a constant in the Galaxy or the Milky Way Coalition would fall to shambles.

The peon standing in the public box reminded him of how grand his life was. Addressing them, the lowly man droned about something or other. Kane was not listening. His mind drifted to the dark, nefarious stare that had the power to destroy the life he built. He was sure that she had no idea what she really possessed. Her perceived ignorance gave him comfort.

The speaker in the box changed. Kane's mind wandered further. How did she find his private vault? Did she know from whom she stole? She had taken so many precautions—evaded every camera, every alarm. She fooled the thermal and the infrared. All of his security never detected her.

The caretaker of his retreat vaguely noticed a moving shadow. Kane flew out there at once. Everything seemed to be in place—until he checked his inner vault. She touched nothing else.

Carefully concealing what she stole, she showed up on Galaxy surveillance footage. Actually, surveillance only scanned half a treacherous eyeball. But, it was enough to identify her.

By the time the Flyers caught Naria, she no longer carried his stolen property. However, Kane had planned for that. When they arrested her, they found rare jewelry from his vault on her. He watched the footage of her arrest enough times to see it in his sleep.

She did not resist. Her dark eyes glared squarely into the Flyers' lenses. "I didn't steal that jewelry. I'm being framed," she said clearly and directly.

Kane watched her trial from the comfort of his darkened high seat. She maintained her innocent story and her cold demeanor. No judge would have proclaimed her innocent. Kane made sure of that. He also had her sent to the most secure prison in the Milky Way, where she was supposed to be tortured for information. Most secure until the breach.

He scowled at whomever voiced a grievance. Not caring what was said, he voted against it.

When he finally returned to his penthouse, he had an extra-long massage session. However, his redheaded android assistant could not ease his mind. She kept trying though. That was one advantage android assistants had over humans.

From his bed, he accessed that day's security feed of his private retreat. His weary eyes could not discern anything new. Dirk had better find her.

He entangled his fingers in synthetic red hair. It felt like silk. Closing his eyes, he allowed it to tickle his skin. He turned off the screen overhead. Relishing her touch, he submitted to the pleasures of synthetic flesh.

Chapter 18

"We're well clear of the Flyers," said Gorm.

"Coordinates?" Wretch asked.

Naria smirked. "Second star to the right and on till morning."

Wretch gave her a strange look. "Sorry?"

"No coordinates. Just fly," Naria said.

"Oh." Wretch understood. "Yes, Captain."

For years, Naria had been a fool. She used her ship as her safe haven, her home. Sure, the Tigerlily transported her across the Galaxy, but she never used it for her acquisitions. And she never allowed her crew to either. She reasoned that it helped maintain the illusion of innocence. In case the ship was ever snared, she did not want evidence in the logs.

She always planet hopped on other ships. Then, she made her final getaway on the Tigerlily. Her crew consisted of loner thieves who came together for a common goal—staying free.

Breaking her out of prison was the first job they did together. They would case targets together or give each other advice or specialized tools, but the job was always a lone one. Her crew was loyal to her. Even the new guy, Rock, seemed okay.

She was ready. The game she had been playing no longer worked. Although some say to change the rules, she decided to change the game.

In the metal corridor, Pistol unlatched her harness. "What has happened to this ship? We need some serious ground time."

"We've all been too busy with our own little projects," said Bob, unlatching his.

"My little project has amassed a small artillery. Or a not so small one," Pistol said, laughing.

"Where is it?" said a voice coming down the corridor.

"Captain," Pistol announced. "Safe."

"Close?" asked Naria.

Standing, Pistol quickly said, "Don't be mad."

Naria smiled. "You've hid it all on the ship."

"I wanted to be prepared," Pistol explained. "I wasn't sure exactly what kind of resistance we'd come up against."

Turning, Naria said, "What about you, Bob? What did you hide all over the ship?"

"Um," he said, plastered to his seat, "stuff."

Naria's laugh echoed off the metal. "We're heading to a safe spot—a junk planet. Evasive maneuvers are not going to work for us anymore. If we're caught, they're not going to do a ship search. They're going to blow us up like space junk. All we have is a blaster for asteroids. I want the Tigerlily well-armed. She needs to defend herself. Pistol, work on the plans. Bob, reinforce our defenses. Rock, come with me."

Slipping off the safety seat, Lorne followed Naria through the corridors. She said nothing until they were safely inside her quarters.

"You did well with Trick," she started. "Now, you said that you're a geologist." Her dark eyes bore into him for a moment. "I acquired some rocks before prison. I need you to examine them. I know you don't have any of the tools of your trade, but we should be able to get them or Gorm can do his best to make them. None of the crew know what I have. Don't tell them. They'll see it for themselves. Make a list of what you'll need." After she dismissed Lorne, she muttered, "I need to know exactly why I am being hunted so fiercely."

Naria remembered landing on the resort planet of Summeret with the tourists. They had their luggage and she had hers. She followed the roads with the groups until she could veer beyond the reach of normal tourists. She knew her path well. She had been stalking the place for months.

Just beyond the perimeter drones of the private estate, Naria had made her base camp. The estate had only one full-time human caretaker—the minimum required. The equipment she left at her base thoroughly scanned the property. The scan told her where every robot, android or otherwise, was stationed. Most of them were kept in storage. Only the security bots stayed active. Her blueprints gave her the full layout of the buildings, including hidden compartments, secret passages, and the vaults.

She knew exactly how to evade the security—the same as the others. Her gear had all the latest and some homemade counter technology. Gorm's greatest talent was breaking through Galaxy security. When nighttime fell, she danced through the estate, working her way to the vaults.

The outer vault opened with one swipe of her hand. She strolled past priceless artifacts, rare ore, art, and gorgeous jewels. It took all her willpower to not snatch the ruby encrusted bib necklace that called to her. Placing one foot in front of the other, she found her way to the inner vault.

She did not breathe as she set the analyzer over the lock's register. The inner vault could only be opened with the vault owner's breath. When the analyzer blinked green, she clicked on the exhale. The device mixed all the signatures it found into a simulated breath.

After the exhale, the vault unlocked. Her gloved hand reached beyond Ion filled stick tabs. Finding a small box, she opened it. Swiping its contents, she left everything the way she found it. No one would notice anything missing until well after she was gone.

Unfortunately, Flyers nabbed her before she could return to the safety of the Tigerlily. She had already secured her small score in the drop point. How stupid she was to think that impersonating a tourist without incriminating evidence would keep the Flyers off her. The evidence they planted on her sat in the outer vault. She knew exactly who arrested her.

"Kane," Naria said to the empty room. He had sent Dirk after her. To be free, she needed to bring him down.

When Naria returned to the bridge, Wretch said, "We'll be coming upon Lumina in three star hours."

"Avoid Lumina," Naria told her. "We're heading for that pink hunk of rock."

The Tigerlily skirted Lumina's space radar. Naria watched the pink junk planet grow bigger on the screen.

"Where should we land?" Wretch asked.

"I'll land," said Naria. "The two of you get everyone suited. The air's barely breathable." She took over the controls while Gorm and Wretch left the bridge.

Naria knew the pink planet well. After coming and going for well over a decade, she could traverse the alien landscape easily. The Tigerlily, however, had only visited a few times. She stopped bringing the Tigerlily so as not to reveal her hideout. Unfortunately, she could no longer hide—at least not within the Galaxy's reach.

The Tigerlily landed in a clearing within a forest of spiky pink rock formations. After quickly slipping on a suit, she joined her crew.

Exiting the ship, their feet touched the sparkling pink dust. Lorne crouched to examine the dirt. Pulverized pink quartz covered the planet.

"We need to manually pull the ship into this cave here," Naria instructed.

Lorne's eyes caught tracks in the dirt. "Schmact," he muttered. The star-like impressions looked familiar and recent. "Captain," he called. "There are tracks here and they're not human."

"I know," said Naria.

Lorne rushed to help pull the ship inside the hanger-like cave. Once the Tigerlily was secure, Naria led them through an airlock in the back wall of the cave. When the indicators turned green, they removed their suits.

She opened a door, which led to a workroom. "Welcome to Beatrice. We can go to and from the ship using breathers. It's best not to go outside without a suit. The caves are breathable. The airlock is just a precaution," Naria told them. "This hideout has food and everything we need. I'd rather not unload the ship. By the way, the Quiquai call Beatrice home. They are tall, bird-like people. They won't harm you, but they may be curious." She stared at Pistol. "Don't shoot them. They may even help us fix the Tigerlily."

"Okay. I won't shoot them," said Pistol.

"Fwhee, aliens!" Bob said.

While the others gathered tools and breathers, Naria motioned for Lorne to follow her. She led him down a lighted tunnel.

"Officially, there is no other life in the Milky Way," Lorne mentioned.

"That's what the Circle would like us to believe," answered Naria. "I was a child on an expedition ship when the expedition found evidence of alien life—plants they thought would be useful as medicine. Not too long after they reported their findings, the ship was attacked. I discovered later that the official cause of the ship's destruction was asteroids." Her grimace almost growled. "Our escape pod crashed here. Most of the escapees stayed with the pod, trying to signal for help. My parents brought me along with their exploration team to see if this planet was survivable.

When we returned to the pod, they were all dead—executed.

"We knew we couldn't trust the Galaxy. After we buried the dead, we scavenged what we could from the pod and brought it into the caves we found. A few days later, we discovered we weren't alone on this planet. The Quiquai saw everything. They took pity on us and taught us how to survive here." She stopped in front of a door with an old combination lock.

As she turned the dial, she continued, "We survivors vowed revenge on the Galaxy. When we were able to get off the planet, we set things in motion. I'm the last survivor."

The lock clicked open. They entered a treasure room. Jewels, gadgets, ore, weapons, ammo, and Lorne did not know what surrounded them. Grabbing a box, she said, "I'm not long for this solar system. All of this goes on the ship."

Naria opened the box. Lorne gazed upon nine intricately cut diamonds. "These supposedly hold data. Can you read it?"

"I'll need a stone analyzer," Lorne said.

"Good. Keep them on you at all times," said Naria. "In the meantime, let's load the Tigerlily with all my acquisitions."

Chapter 19

Dirk buried his tattooed face in his hands while he waited for his food to warm. He was glad that he asked for a bundle of lons for the job. When he heard the beep, he brought his warmed food to the table. Searching each of the junk planets around Lumina was not on his agenda. He would rather pay for his information. But who would trust him if Flyers kept buzzing wherever he went? Like a Ming vase, Bounty Hunting was a delicate art. His contractors failed to understand that. He had to run with the undercurrent, yet be far enough removed to not get burned.

The door opening interrupted his thoughts. Selina entered, giving Dirk a smile. He watched her place food in the cooker. His eyes did not want to rest on her womanly attributes, but they could not help themselves. The way she moved around the galley mesmerized him. His mind drifted to Naria.

Her strength intrigued him. Her ruthlessness should have repelled him, but he found himself drawn closer. She had a mysterious aura that attracted him. She took an interest in his expertise and he willingly shared it. How was he to know that she would rob his client months later?

Selina slid into a chair near him. "This is turning out to be quite the adventure," she said. "Hope it doesn't get us all killed. That would be awful." Her fork lingered on her lips as she ate her food.

"Have you decided where you wanted to go after this?" he asked.

"Some place a miner's daughter can start over," she quipped. "So, do the tattoos mean anything or are they just to hide your tender side?"

He chuckled. "They're old symbols from Earth. The meanings are personal, but mainly death and rebirth."

"You're not what I expected, Dirk," she said. He thought he saw her eyelashes bat.

Scythe walked to the table's edge. "We'll be in Lumina's space radar soon. Are we requesting a dock?" he asked.

"Yes. We are going to resupply while we're there," Dirk answered.

"Would you mind if I searched for work leads?" Selina asked.

"Just make sure you are back on the ship or all your stuff is off by the time we lift off," said Dirk. "Cheat will have the time. If you are not here by the time Cheat says, know that we will not search for you nor come back for you. You will be completely on your own. Understand?"

"Yes... *sir*."

He finished his dinner in silence, feeling as hard and cold as

Naria. At last, he understood her. He had a job to do. Unfortunately, she *was* that job.

As he walked back to his quarters, he did not regret taking the job. If he had not, someone else would have. He had no intention of killing her, not unless he absolutely had to, anyway.

Entering his quarters, Dirk stared at himself in the mirror. The tattoos were post-Naria. He wondered if she would recognize him. Smirking, he figured most likely not.

Knuckles rapped on his door. *Now what?* Opening it, he found Selina on the other side.

She leaned forward, exposing full cleavage. He thought her to be a lot like her mother. "Can I help you with something?" he asked while keeping his eyes from taking a plunge.

Her tongue moistened her lips. "I hope so." She stepped into the doorway, but he would not move. Selina fell into him. Her hands slid onto his shoulders. Her lips rested on his.

Grabbing her waist, he pushed her back. "No, Selina. I have a job to finish."

A finger paused on her bottom lip. "And after?"

He said nothing.

Smiling, she turned. He watched her saunter down the corridor.

Selina was an attractive young woman. None of his crew would have rejected her advances. As he closed his door, he contemplated her agenda.

From his experience, women like her always had an agenda. His ex-wife did. Naria did. Though Naria was worth it.

During the time he spent on her ship, she flirted madly with him. He thought the attraction was genuine. Over a year after his divorce, he sat with Naria in the Dine. She glowed beneath her full head of dark hair as they discussed artifacts.

When he kissed her, he believed she relished it for a second. Pulling away, she said, "I can't. I have something I've gotta finish."

She mostly avoided him after that. Dirk considered himself lucky. The last man who tried to hit on her had his manhood severed with a pen laser. His crotch hurt just thinking about it.

Dirk considered letting Naria go and telling Kane that he could not find her. Whatever she stole could not be that important. He tossed the thought aside. If he failed, he would never work again.

Having Selina on his ship was not good for business. She made him think too much—remember too much. He had to stay focused. His life had to trump.

"Captain, commencing landing procedures for Lumina," said Cheat's voice over the coms.

"I'll be right there," Dirk responded. Glancing at his hardened face in the mirror, he left for the bridge.

Chapter 20

Lorne dumped the last load of Naira's acquisitions onto the table near the airlock. She placed them in appropriate crates. Throwing him a breather, she said, "Let's get all this on the ship."

After affixing their breathers, they carried the first crate through the airlock. The sounds of drilling, welding, and hammering echoed in the cave. Approaching the cargo hatch, Lorne blinked. Working beside the crew were tall, bird-like aliens.

Large taloned feet poked out from underneath long, pink tunics. Each of their four arms ended with three-fingered, talon-like hands. Their eyes and beaks looked similar to pictures of parrots Lorne had seen. Scaly skin covered their faces while colorful feathers adorned the crowns of their heads like human hair.

Naria chuckled at Lorne. "Proof that we are not alone in the Milky Way," she said.

"That's why I went to prison," Lorne mumbled.

They placed the crate in the cargo hold. *Only about a dozen more to go*, Lorne thought as he followed Naria.

A Quiquai walked up the ramp towards them. "Naria, where do I put my stuff?"

"Back home," Naria said.

"You promised." Lorne thought its voice could possibly be female.

Sighing, Naria continued, "Gogi, I'm not coming back."

"I know. In fact, we all know. Please, Naria, let me come with you."

She studied the alien for a moment. "That's Captain Naria to you. Put your bags over there. We'll get you a cabin later. Rock, meet Gogi."

"Hi, Rock," Gogi said excitedly.

"Rock and I are loading crates. You can help," Naria said. She sounded slightly amused.

Inside the airlocked cave, Gogi danced a little as she bent to pick up a crate with her four arms. "My first Pirating adventure," she sang.

"We're being hunted by the Galaxy, Gogi," Naria said as she and Lorne lifted another crate.

"Such is my life," Gogi replied.

As they carried the crates into the ship, Gogi asked, "So, Rock, how did you become a Pirate?"

Lorne never considered himself a Pirate, but such was his life. "I followed the Captain out of Torquor Prison."

"What did you do? Did you kill someone?"

Not believing the delight in her voice, Lorne stared at her.

"Gogi, we don't ask those things," Naria scolded.

Although Lorne was convicted of a multibillion lon theft, he finally understood how he found himself in a dark cell out in nowhere space. "I found evidence of non-human life on a planet whose geology I was analyzing," Lorne admitted. He recalled the talon tracks in the dirt and the bright blue feather. "When I reported it, they sent Galaxy Troops. I had to return to Headquarters. Stupidly, I asked why troops instead of an expedition team. Next thing I knew, I was being arrested in my cabin on Interplanetary Transport."

"Wow," said Gogi.

Shaking her head, Naria responded, "Schmact." She picked up her side of the next crate. "I'd be angrier, if I were you."

Lorne smirked. "I was too scared to be angry. I was supposed to get the sense beaten into me there."

"That explains why you followed me," said Naria. "You're not a criminal—well, you weren't before. And being a scientist, you're more likely to observe than fight the guards."

Naria was right about Lorne. When he shimmied through the small opening in his door, he noticed both Naira and Pistol. He made sure he followed Naria while Pistol set explosives and riled the other prisoners. It was the most daring thing he had done up to that point. He had a feeling that he was in for a lot more daring.

Chapter 21

Early morning sunlight crept along the empty pastel streets. Dirk and Scythe walked purposely before residents and commuters filled the gleaming city of Lucifer. The city had no high rises like Galaxis. Instead, buildings only a few stories high sprawled in every direction for miles. Green space filled the wide gaps between the buildings. Glowing vegetation dimmed in the sun's rays. "Why would anyone want to live on a planet that glows in the dark?" Scythe muttered.

Because of Lumina's natural luminescence, the planet had been touted as the safest planet in the Milky Way. Dirk, however, knew better. Every planet had its share of criminal activity. The underbelly always had a hand that could be greased.

With a reputation of being family friendly, organized crime reveled in Lumina. The governing powers enacted many more laws than on other planets—all in the name of safety. The laws created the crime so prevalent on the planet. All their supposed illegal activities thrived—gambling, alcohol, drugs, and prostitution. The black market swam under the watchful eye of the Patrolbots.

Dirk knew an antique/art dealer from his pre-Bounty Hunting days who moonlighted in black market acquisitions and smuggling. Although he owned shops across the Milky Way, his main shop resided on a pastel street in Lucifer.

A bell rang though the shop when the door opened. An eager young man approached from behind a counter. "What can I help you find today?" he asked.

"I'm looking for Rook. Tell him Dirk's here to see him."

A plump jellybean of a man emerged from a back room. "Dirk! What a surprise. What brings you into my shop?"

"Resupplying the ship," said Dirk. "Thought I'd stop in for a chat with an old friend."

Rook gave Dirk an oily smile. "Come on back," he said. Dirk and Scythe followed him through a door to a back room. "Heard you got out of the business, Dirk. Such a shame. You were one of the best. But, I understand. You got to follow the money."

"Looks like you're doing well," Dirk complimented.

"Can't complain," Rook said. "What is it you need?" He glanced at Scythe. "You don't bring muscle for catching up."

Smiling, Dirk said, "When you need to know something, you are the man to see." He knew exactly how to stroke Rook's overly large ego. "Who would I see for a trip to one of the nearby junk planets?"

"Hmmm," Rook's sausage fingers tapped his round belly. He walked over to a crate. Pulling out a small statue, he placed it on the table. "What do you think?"

No information came free. Studying it, Dirk quickly noticed slight imperfections and an off mark. "Fake. Probably made on Sheena about a year ago."

Rooks face lit. "You are the best. See Shoo in the Blue District. He rents modified transport pods. Tell him you're a friend of mine. He'll give you a good deal."

"Thanks. It was good doing business with you again," Dirk lied.

"If you come across anything good in your travels, think of me first," Rook said as he opened the door.

"Of course." Dirk forced a smile. He and Scythe returned to the pastels.

They jumped onto a Lucifer city shuttle to the Blue District. Scythe turned his head to avoid the ever-present cameras. With his tattooed face, Dirk had no issues with public surveillance. His tattoos wreaked havoc on facial recognition. The only thing he could not fool was the DNA detector. A person tended to leave behind traces of DNA wherever he or she went.

The Galaxy kept a sample of DNA—collected at birth—from every citizen on every planet in the Milky Way. Dirk learned that they never found any of Naria's DNA anywhere. He wanted to know how she attained that feat. He reminded himself to ask her, not that she would spill her secrets to him.

Blue street signs indicated that Dirk and Scythe arrived in the Blue District. With help from the locals, they found the multi-tiered warehouse with a sign reading, "Shoo's Rentals."

They entered a small sales room. Different Transport Pod dioramas dotted the room. "Do you have a reservation?" a cheerful voice asked from behind a counter.

The robot clerk looked to be made out of spare parts from decommissioned transport pods. "No," said Dirk. "We're here to see Shoo."

A door behind the robot opened. "Second door on the left," it said. "Have a good day!"

When Scythe opened the door, about a half dozen heavily armed men greeted them on the other side. "Who sent you?" asked a young man.

"Rook," Dirk answered.

Each man lifted at least one weapon towards them.

Great, Dirk thought. Both he and Scythe showed the men their open palms.

"Rook is a sneak and a cheat," the young man said.

Dirk nodded in agreement. "Yes, yes he is."

The man laughed. "You do not defend him, yet you work for him."

"I work for me," Dirk countered. "Are you Shoo?"

"I am," said a shadow of a man standing in the doorway.

"Grandfather," said the young man. He bowed in respect to the shadow. "I am dealing with Rook's friends."

"He is no friend of Rook," Shoo said. He entered the room with assistance from a cane. "You are the Bounty Hunter known as Dirk. You maintain a relationship with the swindler, Rook, because he pays well and can't cheat you. I would like to know two things. How do the tattoos confuse the cameras and why are you here?"

"Compounds in the ink," Dirk admitted. "I'm here to find Naria."

"Torquor Prison," said the young man.

Shoo raised a hand. "If you are here, then she is no longer imprisoned. Naria is one of my best and oldest customers. Why should I help you?" The old man sat on a chair facing Dirk.

"Because if the Flyers find her before I do, she is dead."

Shoo ordered, "Put down your weapons. We are civilized men." When his guard lowered their guns, he continued, "I propose an information exchange. You tell me how to find the ink. I tell you how to find Naria."

"Deal," said Dirk. At Shoo's insistent look, he said, "Find Freeze on Totem. The design doesn't matter. Make sure you know exactly what you want. No laser removes this ink. Tell her that I recommended you or you won't get the right ink."

Shoo nodded his white haired head. "I don't know where exactly Naria goes," Shoo said. "But I haven't rented the transport she used last since her arrest. We keep old paper logs of the mileage, so we know when the pods need to be maintained. The mileage would be roundtrip from here to wherever and back again. Charlie, the paper logs for lima seven two six."

Without question, Charlie obeyed his grandfather. From a hidden compartment, Charlie extracted a thick, homemade paper. Shoo removed a pair of reading glasses from his pocket. With them perched on his nose, he read the log.

Dirk had never seen either paper or glasses in use. They were artifacts of an old time. Most people had implants to correct their vision.

Looking at Dirk from over his glasses, Shoo said, "I do not trust the Galaxy's implants. According to the mileage, she still travels to Beatrice." The old man smiled. "I personally test flown each modified transport pod to the surrounding junk planets. Beatrice is where I first found Naria as a child—stranded with whomever was left of passengers and crew of a doomed ship. They made a settlement in the mountains. I assisted them with whatever I could. Naria must have kept a base there after the settlement was abandoned. Keep her safe, so she can finish her work."

Taking his cue to leave, Dirk said, "Freeze's services are not cheap. She takes lons and barters." He and Shoo exchanged nods before he and Scythe were ushered through a back door into the streets of the Blue District.

When they returned to the ship, Dirk was disappointed to see Selina still aboard. "Nothing work out?" he asked her.

"Actually, things are looking quite promising," she answered with a smile.

Once the loading hatch closed securely, Dirk took his place on the bridge. "Cheat, take us to a junk planet called Beatrice," he ordered.

Chapter 22

The crew of the Tigerlily sat with the Quiquai in the airlocked section of Naria's cave. Mostly everything on the Tigerlily had been fixed and weapons and shields were added.

"I would like to have some spare parts on hand," said Gorm. They had used everything to mend the ship. "There's nothing left to make an analyzer."

Leaning back in his seat, Lorne sipped the alien liquor their new friends shared with them. "I know where we can get some," he said.

Gorm raised his eyebrows.

"Supposedly, I stole billons of lons worth of equipment from Geo-Terra Headquarters," Lorne admitted. "That place is filled with all sorts of stuff. I might as well do the crime of which I was convicted."

Pistol chuckled.

"Let's set it up," Naria said quietly. "We're on the run. Who's going to expect us to pull off a heist?"

After saying good-bye to the Quiquai, they pulled the Tigerlily out of the cave. The pink quartz sparkled in the night.

Lorne, Pistol, and Bob formed a plan in the Dine while Naria took the controls of the Tigerlily. "There's a place I need to go first," she told Wretch.

She landed near a debris formation in the sand. In a suit, Naria exited the Tigerlily alone. From the bridge, Gogi watched Naria cross the pink landscape.

In the soft pink darkness, Naria found the center of the debris. Her knees collapsed in the dirt. Turning her head, she looked at the carcass of the escape pod. She maintained the memorial to those who had died on the expedition—even those who were not directly slaughtered by the Galaxy. Images of her friends' bodies—other children—left to rot in the intense sun flashed behind her eyes. Those left behind in the escape pod were mostly children. Her parents made her come with them to explore.

The Milky Way killed over half of their expedition. Echoes of screams over the explosions when their ship was attacked rang in her ears. Like all expedition ships and most ships in the Galaxy, their ship had no defenses. The survivors fled into the two escape pods. As their pod fell to Beatrice, she watched a missile hit the other pod. Her heart skipped.

Tears streaked down her cheeks. She could not wipe them through her helmet. "Good-bye," she whispered. "I'm going to avenge you now."

Her hand grazed the markers she placed in the sand for her

friends, then later, her parents. They died from injuries sustained during the initial attack.

"Naria," Gorm's voice called in her ear. "We have movement. A ship is heading straight for us. Captain, run now."

She shook off her tears. One foot followed another as quickly as the suit would allow.

"Captain, they've broken atmosphere," Gorm said.

"She's not going to make it," said Gogi in a panic. She ran out of the ship. Sprinting across the pink sand, Gogi reached Naria in a blur.

"We've been pinged," Gorm bellowed.

Gogi scooped Naria under her arms, then rushed back to the ship in her long strides.

As soon as the airlock closed, Naris barked, "Go!" over the coms. Taking off her suit, she said, "Thanks, Gogi."

The Tigerlily raced towards the stars. "Get close to Dirk's ship," Naria ordered as she entered the bridge. "Give him the thrill of nitro wake turbulence."

"Yes, Captain," said Wretch with a smirk.

Naria's eyes locked on the gray ship.

"Engaging nitrobooster," Wretch announced.

Narrowly, the Tigerlily shot above Dirk's ship. "They're caught in our wake. They won't be following us now," Gorm said.

"Sorry, Dirk," Naria whispered. The Tigerlily sped into space.

Chapter 23

"Schmact!" Cheat screamed. He desperately tried to gain control over the gray ship.

Dirk clicked his harness secure as his ship spiraled to the pink dirt. "Reverse thrusters full blast!" he commanded.

Once the ship stopping spinning, Dirk ordered, "Cut thrusters."

"Brace for a hard landing," Cheat announced.

Slamming into the ground, the ship slid to a stop.

"Run a diagnostic," Dirk said. He removed his harness.

"Where are you going?" Cheat asked.

"Out." Dirk wanted to know why he saw the silhouette of a suit against the pink.

Wearing a suit, he climbed out of the airlock. He approached dark metal spires reaching out of the dirt. Was there something hidden? He unhooked his penetrating scanner from his belt.

Slowly, he scanned the metal. The screen showed names crudely etched on each piece. Groups shared the same surname—families. He turned his scanner to the ground. Human skeletons, most of which were child size, rested below his feet. "Schmact," passed his lips. He stood in the midst of the remains of a doomed ship and the ones who did not survive. She was just remembering the dead. Nothing she stole would have been buried with them.

Dawn broke as he returned to his ship. In the shimmering pink dirt, his eyes caught an impression. Searching the ground, he found more. Long strides came back and forth. A three-taloned footprint was the best he could surmise.

Fear rolled through his body. He hurried back to his ship.

Rushing into the bridge, he said, "Get us off the ground."

"Lift off in two minutes," Cheat said. He turned to Dirk, reading his face. "What's wrong?"

"Something out there is not human," he answered, his voice shaking.

The color drained from Cheat's face. "The ship's repairing as fast as it can."

Shapes approached on the thermal sensors. "We're going to have to repair in space. Go! Now!" Dirk barked.

With a slight pull to the right, they took to the sky.

Chapter 24

Hooded Quiquai watched the gray ship escape Beatrice's atmosphere. Emerging from the pink shadows, they headed to the metal shell memorial. They encircled the memorial, weaving colored ribbons around and between the metal spires.

Once color enclosed the area, they joined hands. In their native language, they chanted. Their words were to protect their old friend, Naria, and their new friends, her crew. They added a protection chant for Gogi, just to cover everyone aboard the Tigerlily. They had already chanted for Gogi on their own hallowed ground.

Disbanding their circle, they returned to the caves before the heat of the day.

Elder Gushock walked through the abandoned human settlement. Ever since their first encounter with humans, all Quiquai had been taught that humans would kill them on sight. Humans had a violent nature and used their advanced weaponry without hesitation on anyone they felt got in their way. Quiquai throughout the galaxy grounded their space travel and kept a reclusive watch.

Many years ago, she saw the human craft crash onto their planet. In fear, they watched. Human families emerged, not soldiers. Bringing only supplies and no weapons, some left to explore—to search for items to keep them alive.

From her shadowed perch, she caught sight of a small ship. She hoped the humans would be rescued and leave them. When it landed next to the wreckage, armed soldiers filed onto the pink sand. Without hesitation, they murdered every one of them, including the children. She would not have believed it if she did not witness it with her own eyes.

Gushock could still hear their wails of despair flooding the mountains.

The slaughter shocked the exploratory party when they returned. She did not know humans had emotions—shed tears, knew love. The humans also knew fear, the same fear the Quiquai knew. Over the course of a week, the humans buried their dead, but kept checking to see it the killers would return. The survivors took refuge in the caves.

After observing the survivors, the Quiquai decided that not all humans were bad and the stranded needed their help. Gushock made first contact.

Although leery at first, the humans welcomed their assistance. They learned. They respected.

Gushock grew to like the humans over the years and considered them friends. Using the Quiquai's anti-Galaxy network, she aided Naria in tracking each of the nine data stones. In exchange,

Naria brought them equipment for their ship that they kept hidden deep beneath Beatrice's pink surface.

With human help, the Quiquai would travel through space again.

Gushock's nostalgic walk brought her to their underground hanger. The large, circular ship was almost ready. It now was outfitted with weapons and defenses to fight against the Flyers and Galaxy Corps.

The progress they made pleased her. Other Quiquai communities across the Milky Way had also improved their ships. They, too, learned that not all humans were their enemy.

The Quiquai knew that they could not fight the Galaxy on their own. Their survival would have to rely on human help.

Their hope rested on Naria's shoulders. She had to succeed.

Gushock wished to see her kind free in her lifetime. The battle for freedom would be a long one. However, her wish was in the beginning stages of fruition.

Chapter 25

The Tigerlily silently stalked Geo-Terra Headquarters. For a remote space quadrant, ships regularly docked and undocked at the well-manned, vast space station. Docking would not have been a problem, however getting through the airlock without proper identification would prove more difficult.

Using Lorne's knowledge of the station, they found another way inside.

Gogi replaced Gorm on the bridge. Bob manned the newly installed defense system. With Wretch positioning the ship under an evacuation chute, Lorne, Naria, Gorm, and Pistol waited by the top airlock.

"Ready," Gogi said over the coms.

With a space belt secured to each of them, Gorm led them out of the Tigerlily. Tethered between Pistol and Naria, Lorne floated in open space for the first time. Gorm overrode the security codes for the round space hatch. They floated inside the corridor, keeping their helmet glass opaque.

The hatch closed. "We're in," Naria quietly told Gogi.

They climbed through an access panel on the chute wall. Gorm perched next to a grid, then released himself from the space belt. He began to infiltrate the wiring. The others kept climbing.

"I'm connected," Gorm said.

Stopping in front of a door, Pistol, Naria, and Lorne detached the space belt.

"Exit in three, two, one," said Gorm.

They climbed into a maintenance room. Pistol immediately stuck a couple of dots on the walls with her thumb. Realizing Lorne watched, she explained, "Just little bombs with remote detonation."

"Okay," Gorm said in their ears. "Surveillance override. Feel free to go."

Slipping out the door, they sneaked down the corridor. "Wait," Gorm told them. They froze. "Okay, go." He watched the three of them approach a storeroom on his hologram.

At the door, Naria placed the delocker over the security pad. When the door slid open, Pistol stunned the guard. He slumped in his chair. She stuck dot bombs near the door.

Lorne knew exactly what he needed. The three of them ran through the shelves, grabbing needed or wanted equipment.

"There's an alarm going off," Gorm warned. His hologram flashed. "Get out! Get out, now!"

Grabbing an analyzing laser, Lorne stuffed it in his bag with the other odds and ends he swiped. He secured his bag to his belt.

"They're coming for you," Gorm said.

"Get back to the ship. We're making our own exit," ordered Naria.

After pulling his equipment, Gorm rushed down the emergency chute.

A series of explosions rocked the space station. Pistol set a large explosive on the far wall. She pressed a button. A significant hole tore through the side of Geo-Terra.

Lorne, Naria, and Pistol got sucked into space along with everything that was not bolted to the floor.

"Engage jets," said Naira. "Try not to hit anything."

Using the panels on the arms of their suits, they wove through debris and bodies. "We have company," said Pistol.

Suited armed guards flew out of the hole. Pistol ducked behind drifting debris to fire her lasers at them. Laboratory equipment shattered around them.

"We need a pick up," Naria called over her coms.

"I see you," said Gogi. "Gorm's on board. We're heading your way."

Lorne's suit flashed brightly, then dulled. The panel on his arm darkened. He could not change direction. "My jets are dead," he said in a panic. He drifted further away from Naria and Pistol. "I think I may have been hit. What do I do?"

He heard nothing.

"Hello? Hello?" Lorne got no answer. "Schmact." He stared into the white dotted black. Inertia would take him or his body somewhere. He could not fight against it.

Something touched his waist. A space belt secured him to either Naria or Pistol. He did not care who saved him, he was just relieved not to be lost in space.

One of them pulled the tandem pair into the Tigerlily's airlock. Lorne unlatched his helmet as soon as the oxygen levels stabilized.

"Pink dots," Gogi's voice carried over the coms.

"Schmact. Flyers," said Pistol. Still in her suit, she ran.

Naria separated her suit from Lorne's. "Thanks," he muttered.

She gave him a nod, then hurried to the bridge. Picking up the bags of what they stole, Lorne brought it all to the Dine.

"Fly us out of here," Naria commanded as she took her seat on the bridge.

Another ship sat in the midst of all the pink dots. Naria's eyes focused on that one ship's dot. "That's gotta be Dirk," she mumbled.

"We're too heavy," yelled Wretch. "Our thrusters aren't turning us fast enough."

More Flyers entered the quadrant.

"Blast us out of here," Naria barked.

"I've always wanted to do this," Pistol said. She aimed at Flyers. The robot controlled ships began to explode.

"We need to nitroboost out of here," said Wretch. "Where to?"

"Where the Flyers can't follow us," said Naria, "Earth."

"Earth?" Wretch repeated. "Outside of Milky Way jurisdiction. Setting course."

"Earth—barren, abandoned, desolate, and depleted—where Pirates go to die," recited Bob.

"Gotcha," Pistol said to her screen. "Rather die on Earth than die here at the hand of the Galaxy."

"We're not going there to die," Naria countered. "We're going there to regroup."

"They're attempting to snare us," Bob announced. "Not sure how long our new shields will last."

"Shoot us a path!" Naria ordered.

Flyers burst into space junk. The Tigerlily fled through space.

Chapter 26

"When did they weaponize?" Cheat asked.

"I don't care! Follow them!" yelled Dirk. They could not travel as fast as the Tigerlily, but the nitrobooster canister would eventually run out of boost.

Surrounded by a flock of Flyers, Dirk shadowed the Tigerlily's trajectory. Cheat flew carefully out of the range of snares. The Tigerlily reappeared on their screen.

"The snares must be slowing them down," Dirk said. "We have a chance."

Pink dots halted their pursuit. "What's going on?" asked Cheat.

Dirk quickly pulled up the quadrant. Spinning the three dimensional hologram, he saw the Flyers' problem. "They're not allowed to leave regulated space quadrants. Fortunately, we can. Keep going."

Chapter 27

After being summoned from a beautiful sleep, Kane ran to Circle Chambers. Inside the cavernous room, a figure stood in the shadows. She stepped into the light when Kane entered. "Your Eminence," Kane said with a bow of his head.

"Thank you for coming so quickly, Kane," she said. "We have a problem."

"How can I help?" he asked.

"I have been alerted of a break in at Geo-Terra. Flyers are in pursuit of a non-regulation black ship believed to belong to one of the Torquor escapees."

Naria, Kane thought.

"Tell me, Kane, is your data stone missing?"

"Yes."

Her Eminence looked around the dark room. "Mine is as well. There are nine stones in all—documenting the formation of the Galaxy Coalition. Each of us keeps a stone safe. The others are checking their stones. Has your hired man recovered yours yet?"

He was not surprised that she knew about Dirk. "Not yet," he answered. "What does this have to do with Geo-Terra?"

"One of their geologists was imprisoned in Torquor for theft," she explained. "He is counted as one of the missing."

Kane felt the color drain from his face.

"You understand the implications," she said.

"I hired the best, Your Eminence. He does not know what he is recovering, but he will recover it."

"I hope so, Kane, for all our sakes. His ship joined the Flyers. It should only be a matter of time. We will convene once all the members of the Circle have returned." She stepped back into the shadows.

Kane's personal android assistant greeted him in his quarters. "What can I do for you, Your Excellency?" she asked.

"Prepare the table. Use the reserve." He watched her obey his orders.

What if Dirk fails? What if Naria proves too elusive? What if this scientist discovers the truth? What will she do with the stones? Could she have gotten all nine?

"Everything is ready." Her smooth android voice interrupted his anxiety.

He positioned himself on the soft sofa. His weary, old bones ached. Galaxy Tower kept him safe from public maladies for many decades. Bending over the table, he noticed his reflection in the glass tabletop. Wisdom lines caressed his face. His skin held up well. He did not look a day over fifty. The serum injections worked on all of them. Her Eminence radiated a youthful beauty—a remarkable feat for one who started on the serum at *her* age.

His eyes switched focus to the lines of white powder waiting for him. Molecularly enhanced fully stimulated the brain. He relished in his recreation of choice. His one hand caressed a tube while the other pressed a finger, closing a nostril. Almost touching the table, he inhaled deeply.

Exhaling, he leaned back. He waited for the euphoria. His brain tingled. Nose to the table, he inhaled again.

The world around him melted. He snapped his fingers. His assistant came running.

"I am a god. Kneel before me."

Chapter 28

The blue planet grew larger on the screen. "We're being followed," said Gogi.

"Let them," said Naria.

"We still have some ammo left in the rear gun," Pistol announced. "I can shoot them."

"Hold your fire. We may need that ammo," Naria said.

The bridge door opened. Gorm entered, saying, "It's built, but we don't have enough power to run it. The snares really damaged us."

Naria nodded. "Great work, Gogi. Gorm, find us a place to land. Bob, take Gogi and Rock and start repairs. Arm everyone where they sit, Pistol."

After the bridge emptied, Gorm asked, "Expecting a fight?"

"I've heard stories of Dirk's brutality," said Naria. She smiled a little. "We need to be prepared."

"He wouldn't shoot you," said Wretch.

"Maybe not," Naria conceded, "but his men might not hesitate to shoot any of you."

Returning with weapons, Pistol gave them each two.

"This can't be," Gorm muttered more to himself than to the bridge. He rechecked his screens.

"What can't be?" asked Naria.

"I'm detecting life," answered Gorm, "on Earth."

"What?" both Pistol and Wretch said, sounding stunned.

"What kind of life?" Naria demanded.

Gorm rubbed his head in disbelief. "Human life. I found a city."

"Power?" Naria continued.

"Yes."

"Land nearby. Make sure we have cover." Naria rose from her seat. "Pistol, keep watch. Let me know when we're going to break atmosphere."

She hurried to the belly of the ship. Poking her head into the engine room, she called, "Gogi, Rock, come with me."

They followed her into the cargo hold. She uncrated a motorbike. "Gogi, you remember how to drive?" Naria asked.

"Of course," said Gogi.

"We don't have enough power, but we are landing near a city."

"On Earth?" Lorne asked.

"When we land, the two of you will take the analyzer and the stones and ride to the city," Naria continued. "Bring the weapons Pistol gave you. If we're right, then what's on those stones will bring down the Galaxy. Dirk, the Bounty Hunter, will land next to us."

"What about you and the others?" Gogi asked.

"We will make sure you aren't followed," Naria said. She placed her hand on Gogi's shoulder. "Some things are worth fighting for."

"Approaching atmosphere," Pistol announced over the coms.

Naria looked from Gogi to Lorne. "Good luck," she said, then walked to the bridge.

Chapter 29

"Is that Earth?" Cheat asked, staring at a blue and white globe.

"Where Pirates go to die," recited Dirk. He watched the black ship glow orange as it descended. "Heat shields must be damaged. They're going to have to repair before taking off again. Land nearby."

Leaving his seat, Dirk walked to the weapon's store. "Captain?" Scythe greeted.

"I need a weapon," Dirk told him. "I'm meeting Naria alone, but armed. The rest of you will wait in case a fire fight breaks out."

Scythe handed Dirk an old, reliable plasma rifle.

Giving Scythe a nod, Dirk slung it over his shoulder. He walked to the hatch to wait for touchdown.

Chapter 30

In the Dine, Lorne gathered the analyzer and connectors in a bag. He met Gogi in the cargo hold. She handed him a helmet, then pulled Quiquai sized goggles over her eyes.

Lorne's heart beat fast as he watched Gogi straddle the motor bike. He climbed on behind her.

The bike sat at the top of the ramp. Lorne checked that his helmet, bag, and gun were secure. Bob pressed a button. Sunlight spilled into the ship when the ramp lowered. The bike roared to life.

The Tigerlily grazed the surface of the Earth. Wretch would not land with the data stones still aboard.

They raced down the barely opened ramp. Lorne held his breath. The bike leapt through the air. Gogi squealed with delight as the tires found earth. The ramp closed behind them. The Tigerlily kept flying.

They rode in the grass around widely spaced trees. Tall, glass buildings shined ahead of them. Peeking over Gogi's shoulder,

Lorne could not believe a city still existed on Earth. He wondered where he could power the analyzer.

A half dozen cars surrounded their bike before they reached the city limits. "Stop where you are!" boomed a voice.

Gogi stopped yards in front of one of the cars. Guns pointed at them from all directions.

An older, dark skinned man stepped out of a car. He stared at Gogi as if he had seen Quiquai before. "What ship?" he asked.

"The Tigerlily," Gogi answered.

"Go!" he told the other cars.

"What do you need?" he asked.

"A power source," Lorne said.

The man nodded. "Follow us."

"A trap?" Gogi quietly asked Lorne.

"I don't think so," answered Lorne. "I think he knows Naria."

The car led them through the grid-like city streets. The city was just as modern as any under Milky Way control. However, Lorne did not see any Patrolbots.

They stopped in front of a large building. Lorne gazed at the modern glass fused to the remnants of an older stone shell.

The man approached. "I'm Frank," he said.

"Lorne and this is Gogi," Lorne introduced as he removed his helmet.

"I thought your name was Rock," Gogi said.

Lorne stepped off the back of the bike. "That's what the Captain named me," he muttered.

"By Captain, I believe you mean Naria," said Frank. Lorne nodded. "Sorry for the less than warm welcome. We don't take kindly to Galaxy scum dropping in on us." He walked them inside large double doors.

"You know Naria?" Gogi asked.

Frank laughed. "I taught her everything she knows. I take it she found what she was looking for. This is the Study Center." He opened a door to a lab like the ones with which Lorne were familiar.

A woman looked up from a nanoscope.

"V will help you with whatever you need," said Frank.

Chapter 31

Wretch carefully landed in the protection of the trees. After taking a deep breath, Naria lowered the cargo ramp. Dirk's gray ship landed beside them. Naria watched the ramp lower. She waited for him in the grass in front of her ship.

He descended the ramp, meeting her in the long grass. "Hello, Dirk," she said. "Nice tattoos."

"Hand over what you stole," he greeted.

"No, hello, how have you been?" she asked.

"Please, Naria, don't make this difficult," he pleaded.

She laughed. "Difficult? Me? The Galaxy has already begun difficult."

"Just give it to me and I'll let you be."

"He didn't tell you, did he?" She chortled through her nose. "You have no idea what you're chasing. You are just going to follow blindly? I thought you were better than that." She stared into his eyes. "He paid you so much you didn't ask questions." She smirked.

"You're free to die here, Naria," Dirk said. "Hand it over."

"Free? Interesting choice of words." She held her stare. "I can't do that."

"And why is that?" asked a female voice from behind Dirk.

"Selina, get back on the ship," Dirk ordered. "This isn't your fight."

Naria's eyebrows briefly raised. The young woman was not Dirk's taste.

Selina descended the ramp with sophisticated flash rifles only available to elite Galaxy Corps. "That's where you're wrong, Dirk. This is my fight." She stopped halfway down the ramp with her rifles pointed at both of them, giving herself the high ground. "I represent Her Eminence. You stole from her as well, Naria."

Naria glared from Dirk to Selina. She laughed. "Men. Clueless every step of the way. Why don't we take a walk and settle this like women?"

"Let's settle this here and now," said Selina. One of her guns fired. Dirk crumpled into the long grass. Selina's other gun pointed directly at Naria's heart. "Don't even think about touching that gun of yours. Hands up. Now."

Reluctantly, Naria raised her hands beside her head.

"Where's the rest of your crew hiding? Her Eminence will be pleased to know that Earth is now inhabitable. Come out, come out, wherever you are!" Selina screamed into the Tigerlily's cargo hold. "Slowly, with your hands up!"

Although breathing hurt, Dirk laid in the grass as quietly as he could. He did not want to draw attention to himself, incase Selina felt like shooting him again.

"Don't go thinking that Dirk's crew is going to come out and save you. I took care of them," Selina boasted.

Footsteps pounded on the ramp. The remaining crew trudged out of the Tigerlily. Their hands were raised, but Naria hoped at least one of them had some sort of plan.

Selina counted the four of them. "Good. Now, where are the data stones?"

"Not here," Naria stated.

Selina pulled the trigger. Gorm dropped. Wretch took a step towards his fallen body. "Don't," Selina warned. She turned to Naria. "Where are they?" she demanded.

"I don't have them," Naria answered.

Gunfire erupted from the flash rifles. Naria and her standing crew scattered. Pain seared in Naria's back and leg. She slammed into the dirt. Her blood stained the surrounding blades of grass.

Pistol touched a button on her sleeve. The Tigerlily's rear gun emptied its chamber. Selina ducked up the gray ship's ramp.

Trying to stay conscious, Naria reached for a blade hidden in her boot. With her remaining strength, she hurled the knife. Selina stumbled off the ramp.

Wretch and Bob rushed to Gorm, Naria, and Dirk. Removing two handguns from her belt behind her back, Pistol strode to where Selina lay. She shot Selina's fancy guns out of reach with her old-fashioned lead bullets.

Seeing Pistol tower over her, Selina clutched her broken leg. "Have mercy," she begged.

"I'll be glad to put you out of your misery," Pistol retorted.

"Tell me, how many have you killed without mercy?"

"I did what I had to do to get away from the mines," Selina answered. "To think my father actually felt sorry for those... aliens."

"You're despicable," Pistol spat.

Engines roared somewhere beyond the ships.

Selina laughed. From her sleeve, she slid a pen laser into her grip. She pressed the end. The laser sliced the barrel of Pistol's left gun.

Pistol allowed a bullet to penetrate Selina's arm.

Selina screamed. "You'll never see the light of day again," she taunted.

"Lower the gun!" a voice yelled across the grass.

Pistol glimpsed armed people surrounding the ships.

Click.

Scorching pain pierced Pistol's rib cage. Finding the gun in Selina's hand, Pistol squeezed the trigger—twice. Two slugs landed in Selina's chest.

Clutching her side, Pistol lowered her gun. She crumpled into someone's arms. "Take the injured to the hospital. Check the ships for others," she heard a voice say.

Chapter 32

"V?" Lorne said. He studied the woman sitting on a high stool. She wore a long, white lab coat over dark clothing. Pinned up hair exposed her graceful neck. Her eyes glimmered with unbridled curiosity.

She nodded. A wispy, light brown tendril kissed V's cheekbone. After pressing a button on the scope, she slid off her stool. She cautiously stepped away from the black topped table.

Lorne noticed her studying Gogi. "I apologize," said V. "I've never met a Quiquai. Since you know Frank, you both must be Space Pirates."

"We are," Gogi said, puffing her feathers.

Lorne held up the analyzer. "I need to power this," he said.

V smiled at him. "Over here," she said. Passing lab stations, she continued, "I'm Vanessa. I run the Study Center Labs. Our main job is to monitor radiation levels. The Earth has done a good job of healing herself, but we need to make sure that we don't add any more radiation or wander into a potentially dangerous area. The long term effect of nuclear radiation is still being realized. The studies done on species left behind are fascinating."

Vanessa led them to an empty table with all the hook-ups he needed. "Have you come to Earth to escape the wrath of the Milky Way? That's why most new arrivals have returned over the past century."

"Depends," Lorne answered as he wired the analyzer to the connections on the table. He retrieved a stone from the pouch around his neck. Leaning in close to the machine, he fit the stone into the facets.

Gogi watched. "How'd you learn all this, *Lorne*?" she asked.

"I have a Doctorate in Geology from the University of Science," Lorne answered while calibrating dials. "However, most of what I know, I learned in the field."

"What kind of field?" Gogi asked.

He glanced at her, then pressed a button. A glow indicated that the analyzer began to work. "In the field means on the job. I learned more studying rocks on different planets than I ever learned in all my years of schooling," Lorne explained.

The contraption darkened. "Come on," he mumbled. He tapped it on the top. It glowed again. "Learned to do that in the field, too."

Lorne peeked through the viewer while the stone spun rapidly. "Do you have a data recorder?" he asked Vanessa.

She placed a flat rectangle on the table. After connecting it to the analyzer, the three of them watched the stone's data on the screen.

"I know the tales, but this is worse," Vanessa commented.

"This is not the history we are taught," Lorne finally said. "And this is only one of nine." He shook his head.

Gogi slowly cascaded onto a nearby stool. "I had heard stories about the annihilation of the Zyne. But that.... My people lie in wait to make their move—retribution for the atrocities committed by the Galaxy. What do *we* do?"

Looking at all the equipment around the lab, Lorne's gaze eventually fell on Vanessa. "We need to make multiple copies."

"We can do that," Vanessa said. "We'll need some help."

Chapter 33

Cheat sat on a bench across from Bob and Wretch. Doctors and nurses filled the operating rooms. The three of them could only wait.

Selina had locked Cheat on the bridge, then disabled all intraship communication. After shooting Scythe in the back, she gassed the rest of the crew.

He rubbed his face. How could he have been so stupid? On Lumina, he caught her communicating with an older woman. She told him that she was checking in with her mother.

The truth, as Cheat began to unfurl it, was that Selina hated her mother, but, obviously, not as much as her father. Her mother, the Madam of the Fox and Hound, got to live and keep her establishment with a surprise inspection from the Galaxy. Her father died in the mine explosion she set to kill all evidence of the alien life on the planet they mined. The kicker—she waited until her father was inside the mine before detonating.

Selina was an agent for the Galaxy. Somehow, she reported

directly to Her Eminence. In her cabin, they found a few stick tabs, weapon prototypes, jewelry, narcotics, and a serum of some sort. The phial was sent to the Study Center Labs for analysis. Their rescuers also confiscated some advanced electronics off her body.

Raising his head, Cheat looked at the rooms holding Dirk and Scythe. The doors did not open. He looked away, but dared not look at Wretch or Bob. He felt responsible for their crew behind the other closed doors.

Bob stood. "You want something to drink?" he asked.

Wretch shook her head.

"What about you?" he asked Cheat.

Surprised, Cheat answered, "No, thanks."

"I can't sit anymore. I'll be back." Bob disappeared down the hall.

The pilots of the two ships sat in an uncomfortable silence. When a door opened, they both looked up.

A man in scrubs approached. "Your Captains are being moved to recovery."

"And the others?" Wretch asked.

"I don't know about them," he said.

"When can we visit?" asked Wretch.

"A nurse will let you know."

Nodding, Wretch sighed in frustration.

"I'm sorry," Cheat blurted.

Lifting her head, Wretch said, "For what? Unknowingly harboring a psychotic agent of the Milky Way Circle?"

"When I first met her, I thought she looked familiar." Cheat beat himself up inside.

"Oh, I'm sure she used her feminine wiles on you bunch," said Wretch, "playing the innocent."

"She tricked her own mother into forcing herself on us," Cheat admitted. He shook his head in disbelief.

"How's your crew?"

"I'm surprised they found Scythe alive after using that thing on him. I'm not even sure what it does. Hopefully, the blood I donated helps," Cheat said. "The others will come to eventually. The gas she used wasn't poisonous. She needed us, not Scythe, to get her back to Galaxis."

"Wretch?" a woman's voice called.

"Yes?" answered Wretch.

"Gorm is asking for you."

Wretch's hand covered her mouth as she stood. "Will he?" Her eyes glistened. She could say nothing more.

"He'll be fine."

"Thank you, Doctor," Wretch breathed.

Gorm laid on a bed with his torso elevated. Holographic monitors floated over his head. Spotting Wretch, he smiled. His hand reached for hers. "Walk with me to recovery?" he asked.

She slid her hand into his. Squeezing it slightly, she expressed her gratefulness that he was alive.

Bob returned to the waiting room to find only Cheat. "What happened?" Bob asked.

Before Cheat could answer, a nurse said, "Your Captains are awake. You can see them now."

The men followed the nurse into a large room. Wretch was already there with Gorm. Dirk and Naria watched the newcomers enter.

"Where's Pistol?" Naria asked.

"Still in surgery," Bob answered.

Cheat informed Dirk of their crew's status.

"And Selina?" Dirk asked.

"Dead," said a man's voice from the doorway.

Naria's eyes snapped in the direction of the voice she recognized. She saw an older version of a face she grew up knowing well. "Frank," she said. "I thought you were dead."

"I hope the rumors are greatly exaggerated," Frank said with a wry smile. "Imagine my surprise when I escaped to Earth and found civilization." He entered with Gogi trailing behind him.

Dirk and Cheat stared at the Quiquai as she approached Naria's bed. "The ships have been towed into dock," Gogi reported. "Frank informed us about the shootout." She spied Dirk in the next bed. "What's *he* doing here?"

"We're all on the same side, Gogi," Naria said. "Where's Rock?"

"Rock or Lorne or whatever his name is had five of nine copied when I left with Frank."

"Will it work? Is it as bad as we thought?" Naria asked. She needed to know if getting shot was worth it.

"Worse," replied Gogi. "The battles for certain planets and extinctions of entire peoples splatter Milk Way history."

"No one is going to care about that," Dirk chimed in. All eyes fell on him. "Oh, come on. Don't look at me like that. Most people are completely self-absorbed. If it doesn't affect them now, they don't care. And they won't budge a muscle to overthrow the Circle." He looked at Naria's raised eyebrows. "I know that's what you want. I saw the memorial on Beatrice. I'm sure the travesty happened at the hand of the Galaxy."

"People will care about the cures for diseases that are being kept from them," Lorne said when he joined the recovery room. "Only a select few benefit from alien technology and medicine. And then there's the Ageless Serum. We determined that Ageless Serum was in the phial found in Selina's cabin. Ageless Serum is real reason the Galaxy collects our DNA at birth. If a baby's DNA has certain markers, it is plucked from the hospital. The parents are told that it died, but it is brought to a facility where its blood, stem cells, and bone marrow are harvested to create Ageless Serum for the Circle. No child survives beyond the age of three."

Lorne heard sharp intakes of breath, but no one spoke. He removed the stone filled pouch from around his neck. Holding it towards Naria, he said, "Multiple copies are being made."

"Keep the originals until we find a safe place to store them," she said. "We need to figure out how to use this info to our advantage without getting caught."

"Can you make fakes?" Dirk asked.

Lorne nodded.

Smiling, Dirk said, "I have an idea."

Chapter 34

From his hoverchair, Scythe directed the transfer of items from Dirk's ship to the Tigerlily. A small army unloaded, loaded, and repaired the ships. Dirk watched from the space dock with a pang in his stomach. He purposefully did not name his ship so that he would not become attached to it. He would not sigh while standing next to Naria.

"Are you sure you're okay with this?" Naria asked him.

"My final payment was supposed to be your ship," he said. He had said his farewells to his ship when he removed his accumulated personal belongings.

"My ship?" She stared at him. "For the memories?"

Dirk shrugged.

Shaking her head, Naria watched Gorm and Bob roll a homemade machine up the ramp of Dirk's ship.

"Dirk," called Lorne. The geologist handed him a pouch. When Dirk examined one of the stones, Lorne said, "Just some random data."

Light shined on the clear stone, posing as a stolen data stone. A couple of days prior, Naria borrowed a truck from Frank. No one flew transport pods around Earth. They did not want the Galaxy detecting any advancement on the abandoned planet. She scoured the land for a decent hiding place that she would stake for her very own. When she found it, she buried the original data stones. In her and Dirk's plan, they would use the copies Lorne made.

"Good job," Dirk commended. He took a deep breath.

"Everything's done," Scythe told Dirk and Naria. "Wish I could be of more help. I'd like to see Her Eminence get hers."

Dirk shook Scythe's hand. "Thanks, Scythe. You'll be walking around by the time we get back."

Scythe hovered to the other side of the red safety line. The Tigerlily's crew plus Dirk and Cheat approached the ships.

"Lorne." Vanessa ran onto the landing pad. "For luck." She pressed a smooth rock into his hand.

Black granite rested on his palm. A *V* was chiseled in the center. When he looked at her, she smiled, then ran behind the line.

Nudging him, Bob said, "Fwhee."

Lorne smiled despite possibly flying to his doom. He gazed at her light brown hair framing her face. He had someone to come back to.

Cheat and Gorm separated from the group, walking up the ramp of Dirk's ship. The rest entered the Tigerlily.

From the bridge, Dirk watched his ship lift off without him. When it disappeared from view, he stood against the wall with Lorne.

"They broke atmosphere," Gogi announced.

With Pistol and Bob manning the weapons and defenses controls, Naria said from her Captain's chair, "Wretch, let's finish this."

"Yes, Captain," Wretch said. The black ship roared into the blue sky.

Blue morphed into black. "Gogi, send the message."

Honing into the correct frequency, Gogi spoke in her native tongue. She listened to the channel for a response.

"Elder Gushock is replying," Gogi said, a little surprised. "They'll be waiting for the signal." She looked over her shoulder at Naria. "It won't just be the Quiquai. Other peoples have banded together to join the resistance. And some humans, too."

"Excellent." Naria smiled.

The Tigerlily eventually slowed to avoid the space traffic buzzing around Milk—the milky white planet housing Galaxis and the Milky Way Circle.

"Gorm's requesting open coms," said Gogi. Naria gave her a nod. "Go ahead, Gorm."

"Captain, we're in orbit around Milk," said Gorm's voice. "We've lassoed the main satellite. Data download is on schedule. Will be disabling secure coms. Transmission will begin on time."

"Good. See you on the other side," Naria said.

"We'll be awaiting pick-up."

The bridge silenced. They watched the countdown clock tick away on the screen.

Wretch burned the thrusters just enough to begin the Tigerlily's float towards Milk.

When the clock hit zero, Naria stood. Her eyes found Dirk. "You're up," she said.

Passing Naria on the bridge, Dirk wanted to reach for her. He dared not. They may have laughed and lowered their guards while recovering on Earth, but they were in the middle of the job she needed to finish. He sat in her chair determined to make his plan work.

"Gogi," he ordered, "connect me with charlie hotel echo kilo. Use code seven niner delta."

"Connecting. Keeping coms open," Gogi responded.

Chapter 35

The Circle reconvened when the last of the dignitaries returned to Galaxy Tower. Kane wondered for how long Naria had been after the stones. She stole every one of the nine data stones. The other dignitaries never noticed that his or her stone was missing.

Her Eminence spoke in her disdainful voice about how she employed one of her agents to retrieve the stones. Kane tuned her out. He had enough of her accusatory tone and reproachful glares. Privately, he hoped that her agent would fail. He wanted his hired man, Dirk, to succeed.

The other dignitaries hovered in their spots. Some winced with each scolding word. A light on Kane's wrist messenger tore his attention from the lecturing drone. He read the incoming sequence. "Excuse me, Your Eminence," he interrupted.

"What is it, Kane?" She sounded annoyed.

"My man has just contacted me."

Finally, she stopped her condescendence. Her eyebrows

raised. "Put him on hologram for all of us to see and hear." Her eyes narrowed. "I hope this is good news."

Kane swiped his thumb across his messenger. Dirk's holographic image appeared slightly above the MWG emblem, yet still well below the dignitaries' floating perches. His face scrambled and flickered every so often. The holographic transmitter did not take kindly to Dirk's tattoos. "Dirk, welcome to the Galaxy Circle," Kane said, trying to irritate Her Eminence. "You are in front of the full Circle. What news have you?"

Dirk's eyes swept around the room. "Your Eminence and Your Excellencies," Dirk said as his head bowed respectfully. "I have recovered what was stolen."

Some of the dignitaries relaxed while others stiffened, more on edge.

"Show us," ordered Kane.

The Circle peered at him eagerly.

Dirk held a dark pouch up for all to see. Turning it over, nine large diamonds cascaded into his hand. He held one between his fingers. When the light pierced the facets, Kane noticed the telltale data marks inside the stone. A few breaths escaped around the Circle. He returned the stones to the safety of the pouch.

"Well done," Kane praised. "Did you receive your final payment?"

Smiling, Dirk said, "It is better than expected."

"Mister Dirk, if I may," Her Eminence hijacked the conversation.

Dirk turned his full attention to the older woman trying to float slightly higher than the others.

"You had a young woman aboard your ship, I believe. Is she around?" she asked.

"If you are speaking about Selina, I am sorry to report that she did not survive the encounter with the Pirates," Dirk said, lowering his eyes.

Her Eminence's jaw stiffened.

"Was there a big battle?" Emmery interjected.

"Yes, Your Excellency. It was not pretty and I will spare you the gory details," Dirk said.

"And what of Naria?" asked Kane.

Dirk shook his head. "She was shot," he answered.

"What happened to the scientist?" Her Eminence asked.

"The scientist?" Dirk repeated.

"We have reason to believe Naria had a scientist aboard her ship," Her Eminence clarified.

"Many were lost," replied Dirk. "Since no scientist was taken prisoner, I must believe that he was as well."

Her Eminence gave Dirk a smile. "We will reward you well for your efforts, Dirk," she said. "You have permission to land your ship atop Galaxy Tower."

"Thank you, Your Eminence," Dirk said with a bow. His hologram blinked.

"Greetings, citizens of the Milky Way Galaxy," bellowed Naria's voice through every communication device. "Their Esteemed Excellencies and Eminence of the Milky Way Circle have lied to us. But don't take the word of some fugitive Space Pirate. See the proof for yourselves."

Dirk's hologram disappeared.

"Where is he?" Her Eminence shouted. "Find the source of that transmission!"

Chapter 36

"Go! Go! Go!" Dirk yelled.

Wretch fully engaged the thrusters. Dirk's ship blinked on the screen.

"They might need a hand," Naria told Lorne. "Use the claw."

Dirk followed Lorne into the belly of the ship. Quickly, they stepped into suits. "I'll get the claw into position. You get the doors," said Lorne. "Activate boots. I'm throwing us into zero gravity."

"We're coming upon them," Gogi said.

Lorne turned wheels while Dirk shifted levers. Their boots kept them attached to the floor when the doors opened. The momentum carried the claw down the chute. Watching the rope, Lorne waited for movement.

The rope hit the side. Peering through the hole in the floor, Lorne saw two helmets. Their hands clutched the rope. Their boots rested on the claw.

He turned the wheel. The claw rose into the belly of the ship.

Dirk closed the doors to space.

Hitting a switch, Gorm returned pressure to the room. They removed their helmets. "All aboard and ready to go," Gorm said into the coms.

"Copy that," said Gogi.

The ship scurried far from Milk yet close enough to keep watch.

Returning to the bridge, Gorm said, "That data is being broadcast to every corner of the Galaxy. There is nothing they can do to stop it." He smirked.

"Flyers are going to be searching for us," said Dirk.

"Come and get us," Gorm taunted.

"They found Dirk's ship," Gogi said.

Dirk's gray ship waited in orbit for the white missiles launched from Milk. Impact brought a series of fireballs. Only gray debris remained.

With his ship reduced to rubble, Dirk felt a pang of loss. He had never intended to keep the ship. He only had it until he could afford something better. Yet, when he could, he decided not to part with it. Why spend money to replace a perfectly good ship? "Are you no longer a captain if you don't have a ship?" he mumbled.

"All nonessential ships have been grounded. The quadrants are filling with Flyers," said Gogi. She searched her screens. "Where are they? We're alone in a sea of Flyers."

"We can only worry about us right now," Naria said. "Stations, boys."

While on Earth, they practiced reloading their weapons.

Lorne, Dirk, Gorm, and Cheat took their positions in the different parts of the ship. Tethering themselves to the walls, they were ready for any evasive maneuvers Wretch would employ.

"I see one! And another!" Gogi exclaimed. "Oh my! There's a whole bunch of ships."

"Any Galaxy Corps?" Pistol asked.

"No. They'll lead with their Flyers," said Wretch. "To see what happens."

"Let's send these Flyers to the scrap heap," Naira said. "Harnesses." When the clicks subsided, she said, "Lock your targets and take your first shot."

Pistol fired three of the guns at once. Flyers burst around them.

"They're locking on," warned Bob.

Wretch flew the Tigerlily forward, then flipped upside down, going under and back. Pistol struck two more.

Within the quadrant, Flyers exploded. Other ships joined the firefight.

Pistol found her targets while Wretch weaved and bobbed. The robot operated ships disintegrated into space junk.

"I'm picking up a distress call," said Gogi. "A Quiquai ship has been hit. Its crew is floating. They are requesting a pickup."

Naria nodded.

"There's one near the cargo hatch," said Gogi.

"I'm closest," said Dirk over the coms. "I'll suit up."

Gogi notified the floater in her native tongue.

In a suit, Dirk activated his gravity boots, then released the pressure in the cargo bay. He opened the ramp just enough for someone to float inside. Walking to the opening, he spotted the four-armed light suit against the darkness. Two of the arms held an unconscious someone with two arms.

"We're going to need medical assistance," Dirk announced. He tied himself to the inside of the ship. His boots found the ramp's edge. Stretching out his arms, he helped bring the two inside the ship.

The Quiquai spoke to Dirk in his native language.

"I don't know what you're saying," Dirk replied, shaking his head.

The alien pointed into space.

Another Quiquai drifted, unable to move. Fear filled his bird-like face.

"Schmact," said Dirk. "I'm going out for another," he told whomever was listening. After checking the security cable, he opened a panel in the wall. He handed a photon blaster to the Quiquai, then took a plasma cannon for himself.

Suited crewmembers helped the injured one out of the cargo hold. As the Quiquai positioned himself near the opening, Dirk pushed off the outside of the ship. Using the jets on the back of his suit, he flew to the stranded Quiquai.

He securely clipped the alien's suit to his. Slowly following the security cord, they jetted towards the Tigerlily.

A laser cut the tether. Using the jets, Dirk positioned them directly between the Tigerlily and the Flyer. He aimed the plasma cannon, then pulled the trigger.

A light blue stream pierced the Flyer. The force of the stream propelled them into the Tigerlily. Another ship's fire finished the Flyer.

The cargo ramp closed. Someone in a suit righted the immobilized Quiquai, then unlatched him from Dirk. When the pressure returned, the other Quiquai helped remove suits.

Helmets off, the Quiquai spoke to each other in their language. Dirk glanced at Naria in the other suit.

"Thank you for rescuing us," said the second Quiquai. "I am Faroe. Maque does not speak Human. He would like to know the status of the Tzatza he brought aboard."

"Welcome to the Tigerlily, fellas," said Naria. "We took his friend to the infirmary. Maque is free to check on him."

Free of their suits, Dirk returned to his station while Naira brought the Quiquai to the infirmary. Lorne tended to the Tzatza whose skeletal body was reminiscent of an Aztecan deity. The alien drank something Lorne gave him.

"That should start healing me," said the Tzatza. "Thank you for making it." Its glowing eyes found Maque. "I would be dead if it weren't for you."

Faroe translated. After listening to Maque's response, he said, "We are all on the same side. We leave no one to die."

"Rest and heal," Naria said to the Tzatza. "Doctor Lorne, here, will watch over you."

Hearing her use his real name, Lorne's head snapped to look at her. He raised his eyebrows at the doctor moniker. She gave him a smile, then took the Quiquai to the bridge.

Faroe and Maque stared at Gogi in the navigator's seat.

"Flyers are approaching from all surrounding quadrants," she announced.

"Reposition," said Naria. "Wretch, I defer to your expertise."

"Yes, Captain," Wretch said.

"Captain," said Gogi, "there is other movement in the quadrant. Small ships leaving Milk."

"Put it on the screen," Naria ordered.

Small, charcoal colored, diamond shaped ships filled the screen.

"Schmact. Galaxy Corps," said Wretch. "Wait a minute. I only count fifteen. Gogi, confirm."

"Fifteen confirmed," said Gogi.

"Odd," muttered Wretch. "A proper formation is thirty."

A blast from another ship broke the formation.

"They're attempting communication," said Gogi.

"Put it through," said Naria.

"Hold your fire! I repeat, hold your fire," said a voice. "This is squad leader G. C. ... Forget it. This is Vapor. We have broken from Galaxy Corps. The fight is with the surrounding Flyers." The voice paused. "Anyone copy?"

"Fine with me, Vapor," Wretch answered. "Just stay out of our way. And, if any of your squad decides to play both sides, they will be terminated. Do *you* copy?"

"We copy," said Vapor. "Wretch?"

"That's First Commander Wretch to you, Vapor," she said. "Now, there are Flyers out there that want to be junked. If you're in this fight, get shooting."

The formation scattered in synchronization.

"Ammo is low in guns three and five," said Pistol.

"Rock's doing the doctor thing," Naria said. "He had to leave his post."

"We can reload," offered Faroe.

Naria gave them a nod. She brought them to Lorne's abandoned station.

As soon as Galaxy Resistance demolished a Flyer, another took its place. An endless horde of Flyers wreaked havoc on the Resistance.

"I'm running out of cartridges for guns four and six," Cheat said over the coms.

"I was afraid of that," Pistol muttered. "Let me know when you load the last in each gun." After ridding the Galaxy of a few more Flyers, she said, "We may need to shoot from the airlocks."

A Galaxy Corps ship sped over the Tigerlily, spiraling out of a Flyer's snare.

Wretch flew the Tigerlily through the path Pistol blasted to the far corner of the quadrant. The addition of the rogue Galaxy Corps reduced the number of Flyers protecting the Galaxy Coalition.

"More Galaxy Corps are leaving Milk," Gogi said.

Watching the mass of ships in formation, Wretch asked, "How many shots do we have left?"

"About ten in each gun, if I don't miss," Pistol answered.

"Eighty," Wretch counted. "How are our defenses holding?"

"Pretty well," replied Bob.

"Then, let's play chicken," Wretch said with a smile. "Pistol, shoot nothing until we're within their formation. Those ships are built for speed and maneuverability. They pierce easily. I'm surprised they don't burn up upon reentry."

"So, they're schmact," said Pistol.

"Nowhere near as tough as a Flyer," Wretch said.

"Gorm," Pistol said over the coms, "recalibrate to shoot half power."

"All of them?" asked Gorm.

"Nah. Leave seven and eight. A girl's gotta have some fun."

Half power meant that Pistol could take two shots for every one at full power. Looking at the formation, Naria knew it would still not be enough. She sneaked out of the bridge.

When she peeked inside the infirmary, the Tzatza said, "Captain, I presume?"

Naria gave him a nod. "You may wish to strap yourself in. We will be taking a few turns," she told the alien. "Rock, come with me."

Lorne walked with Naria into the corridor. "Bring the Quiquai we rescued to the cargo hold," she instructed.

Dirk was already half suited when Naria arrived with Cheat. "Read my mind," Naria told him. Once Lorne brought both Quiquai men, she said, "Faroe, your suit is beyond repair. In the crate behind you, you'll find a Quiquai suit. Everyone, suit up and activate your boots. When the guns are out, we're left. Two to an airlock."

Suits secure, Naria passed around hefty photon and plasma cannons. She snapped a space case around a large caliber, old-fashioned, semi-automatic rifle. Bringing extra clips, she and Dirk walked to an airlock.

The waiting teams braced themselves against the walls as the Tigerlily twisted and turned through space. Peeking through the porthole, Lorne watched charcoal diamonds blow up in chain reactions. He leaned against the wall and closed his eyes.

"First time?" Cheat asked.

Lorne opened his eyes. "What?"

"Using a gun."

"Is it that obvious?"

Cheat laughed. "I used to be an Interplanetary Transport pilot. Developed a taste for gambling in my downtime. Someone accused me of cheating. Had to settle the argument with a duel. It was the first time I ever laid hands on a gun. The first time you pull the trigger is the hardest."

Lorne nodded. "What happened with the dual?"

"I won." Cheat smirked. "Been called Cheat ever since."

He did not really want to know the details. Lorne took some deep breaths. Although he could feel Vanessa's gift in his pocket, he hoped that they would not have to open the door to space.

Chapter 37

"What do you mean you can't shut it down?" Her Eminence bellowed.

A man's hologram bore the wrath of the Galaxy Circle. "The broadcast is like a virus. It keeps spreading," he explained. "The harder we try to contain it, the faster it spreads. It's overriding everything." His hologram blinked. "I don't even know how long I can keep this communication open."

"This is a secure channel," said Her Eminence.

"Security doesn't—" The man disappeared. The data from the stones took over.

"Get! That! OFF!" she screamed.

A woman ran inside the chamber. "I can't close the channels," she told them.

The nine crashed to the floor.

Horrified, the woman mumbled, "I need to get out of here." She scurried from the room, ignoring the fallen dignitaries.

Chapter 38

Pistol laughed with maniacal glee. With Wretch's superb flying, she was able to hit multiple Galaxy Corps ships with one shot. "Guns four and five are done," she announced.

The Tigerlily twisted while coiling through the Galaxy Corps formation. Charcoal ships splintered in the speckled black.

"There go seven," said Pistol, "and two." She fired judiciously, carefully measuring each shot for maximum damage.

After relishing the explosive aftermath of her handiwork, she said, "I'm out. Time to use the Baby." Pistol left the bridge to put on her suit.

"That's it, guys. Fire at will," Wretch said over the coms. "I'll try to get you good shots."

Three doors to space opened. Wretch rolled through the Galaxy Corps. Dirk and Naria took turns shooting at passing ships. Cover being sparse, they relied on Wretch's flying.

Cheat took his shot, which crippled a Galaxy Corps ship. Lorne's heart raced, knowing it was his turn. Although he had been holding it for what seemed like an eternity, the gun still felt foreign in his hands.

He inhaled deeply. The barrel of his gun pointed at a charcoal diamond. His gloved finger gently tapped the trigger. Two ships erupted into fiery debris.

"Nice shooting," Cheat said as he lined up his next target.

Lorne smiled. He finally felt like Rock.

In the cargo hold, Pistol uncrated what she called, the Baby. She cradled the laser guided photon missile launcher as she attached the wide body to the tripod. After clamping the tripod to the ramp, she opened the back hatch just enough to fire.

Peering through the scope, she locked on her target. Her finger pressed a button. The Baby discharged. While the missile met its target, she scoped the next one.

Clearing the Galaxy's ships was slower without the Tigerlily's guns, even with Gorm using his modified cannon through the belly hatch. The Tigerlily sustained blow after blow. Wretch only evaded the most direct Galaxy strikes.

At the port airlock, Cheat moved to the opening for his shot. A metal rope tendril wrapped around his torso. At the other end of the tendril, a charcoal ship tried to tug him into space.

Lorne drew a pen laser from his suit. With one hand clutching a handle by the door, his thumb depressed the top button. The laser chipped through the metal rope.

Cheat pulled himself into the Tigerlily, allowing his gun to float away. The pen laser finally gnawed through the tendril. The metal rope whiplashed into the Galaxy Corps ship.

While avoiding one hit, the Tigerlily rolled into another.

Gorm grabbed onto the claw to keep himself inside. The lights flickered throughout the ship.

"Defenses are down. We're losing power," Bob said.

Closing the belly's hatch, Gorm sprinted to the engine room.

"Conserve power. Cut coms," ordered Naria.

"I'll create a diversion if Wretch can fly out of here," Pistol said.

"Pistol, wait," Naria called. She heard nothing beyond the dampened sound in her ear.

Dirk motioned for Naria to go. He could shoot solo for a while. She ran through emergency light illuminated corridors. When she reached the cargo hold, she stopped near the ramp.

Pistol stood on the ramp's edge. She held a static rifle in each hand. Weapons ensconced her suit. Seeing Naria, Pistol saluted. Arms extended, she pushed off the spiraling Tigerlily into space.

"Pistol! Pistol!" No one heard Naria's screams. She watched Pistol shoot into the darkness. The Tigerlily sped away from her. Pistol faded into the black.

"Captain," Gogi said in her ear. The coms returned.

"Pistol jumped. Go back for her. Go back!" yelled Naria.

"Captain, we can't," Gogi said in a soft voice. "Controls are gone."

Tears leaked down Naria's face. She remembered first meeting Pistol in a black market weapons shop. Naria shopped for her first gun.

"You don't want that one," Pistol told her from across the aisle.

Naria held the zap blaster in her hands. "Why not?"

"Slow reload and the firing rate is unreliable," Pistol said matter-of-factly. She approached Naria. "For personal use, go with a photon pistol and an old-fashioned revolver as a backup. Oh, and do you have a pen laser? Super useful."

Naria took her suggestions. They browsed other shops. After bonding over losing loved ones at the Galaxy's hand, Pistol became the first crewmember of the Tigerlily.

"Captain? Captain?" Gogi interrupted. "What now?"

Naria stared into the black expanse. "Are we moving?" she asked.

"We're caught in a planet's gravitational pull," explained Wretch. "Once we break atmosphere, we will crash."

Her crew depended on her. She breathed deeply. "Secure all airlocks. Shut everything down except life support. That includes gravity. Everyone wears a suit. Gather in the cargo bay," instructed Naria.

She took a final gaze out into space. "Good-bye, Pistol," she whispered. She closed the ramp.

When the oxygen level returned to normal, she removed her helmet. To conserve her suit's energy, Naria flipped off her gravity boots. Floating, she waited for the others.

As the crew entered, she counted. Six humans. Three Quiquai. One Tzatza. "We're going down. We may need to jump," she told them.

Silently, everyone hovered over crates, waiting.

"You okay?" Dirk asked her quietly.

"I will be," Naria answered. She closed her eyes. Behind her eyelids, her parents smiled. She rightly avenged them.

Her head kissed the ceiling of the Tigerlily. She remembered rummaging through a scrap yard. "Hey, Frank," she called. "What do you think of this?"

Buried in the trash sat the Tigerlily. The gray hull had a dull non-finish. An old numbering system flaked off the side. Its sleek body stirred her sense of adventure. Parts may had been rusted, but the bones were good.

Standing next to her, Frank said, "I think you found a beauty." He clapped her on the shoulder. "Let's dig her out and see what she needs."

They worked tirelessly for months rebuilding and improving the ship. Frank helped Naria salvage parts and steal bits and pieces of whatever they needed to finish the job. Giving the Tigerlily advanced modern technology reassured Naria that she had found the right ship for her mission. Restoring a relic was a slow conquer. The two of them finished one area before tackling another.

"Well, what do you know," said Frank while working on the control panel. Naria left the navigation console to admire a stick springing from under the controls.

"What is it?" she asked.

"Manual override," Frank explained. "Any ship built within the last thirty years does without this. A stupid choice, in my opinion. The yolk won't let you fly it too well, but you'll land her."

Naria opened her eyes. The Tigerlily buffeted while entering atmosphere. "Hold on to something. Gravity will be returning with a vengeance," she warned.

They reached for the floor before it met them. The shaking ceased. Gravity returned. "Open the extenders. It will slow our rate of descent," Naria ordered. Taking her helmet, she ran to the bridge.

Under the control panel, she flipped a switch. A single sticked yolk popped in front of her. "Glide her," she heard Frank's smooth voice say.

A craggy landscape stretched underneath her. "I need a place to land," she muttered.

"May I, Captain?" asked the Tzatza.

Naria nodded. "Can you see a good spot?"

"I believe this to be Ixapolcal, my people's home planet," said the Tzatza. "If the poems are true, then the folded mountains give way to bright fields." He studied the landscape from the window. "There! Just beyond. Keep heading towards the horizon."

Naria willed the Tigerlily to keep altitude. The cargo compartment challenged gliding. When she bonded the hematite to the hull, she discovered that the entire expandable cargo bay splits from the ship. A large parachute would let it softly float to the ground.

Releasing it over the wrinkly landscape would be unwise. They had to hope for a gentler crash landing. Finally, she spied a golden field.

The ground rapidly approached. Naria could do nothing to slow the ship. "Brace for impact," she said.

The Tzatza harnessed himself in the navigator's seat.

Landing gear slammed into the field. The Tigerlily dug a path through the golden vegetation. Friction eventually halted the forward momentum.

She and the Tzatza rushed to the cargo bay. After learning that everyone survived, Naria said, "Let's get the core fixed as soon as possible."

"Should we send out a distress signal?" Wretch asked.

"War rages. Who is going to answer?" Naria asked in return.

Donning helmets, Naria and Bob scurried outside to assess the damage. Gorm brought Lorne with him to the engine room.

Gold dust smeared the black underside. The landing gear was wedged in light brown mud. Appearing from the other side of the ship, Bob gave her a thumbs-up. They walked towards the airlock to retrieve a couple of shovels.

"Stop where you are and put your hands up," said a voice behind them.

Great, thought Naria. The one time she left her ship without her gun, someone poked a barrel into her back.

She and Bob waded through the golden grass. Her crew stood ahead of them, surrounded by armed Tzatza. She counted. Two were missing. She hoped Gorm and Lorne were still on the ship alive.

Once they joined the others, the armed Tzatza paraded them away from the Tigerlily.

Chapter 39

Groans reverberated off the smooth marble walls of Circle Chambers. "What happened?" Emmery asked. She rubbed her hip while still lying on the hard floor.

"The Equalift faltered," someone answered.

Emmery's face scrunched. "Obviously." Her terse tone cut through the circle.

Some dignitaries did not dare move. They waited for someone else to pull them off the floor. Others slid against the wall for support. They were not as young as they pretended to be. Bones hurt. They were used to being pampered.

"Oscar, get in here," Her Eminence ordered into her wrist messenger. "Oscar! Get. In. Here. Now!"

"I don't think they can hear us," one of the Circle said.

"Of course not!" Her Eminence threw back at him. "I can't believe I have to suffer for your lax security. Shouldn't take too long for me to get this under control."

"Your stone was stolen as well," said Kane.

"At least I was doing something about it," Her Eminence snapped.

Her agent, Selina, piggybacked on his hired man. Kane pushed himself onto his knees. "Her being dead doesn't help us any," he retorted. His body ached. Although his muscles protested, he wobbled to his feet.

"Your man turned on you." Her eyes became slits.

"So he did." Kane stepped on top of the emblem. "It's over, Julia." Her Eminence gasped at the use of her name. "I don't have any grand disillusions that this can be restored. They'll be at our doors soon enough, if they're not already here." Turning from the stunned Circle, he strolled out of Chambers.

Kane entered his penthouse, hoping his assistant still worked.

"Your Excellency," his redheaded android greeted.

"Prepare the best," he said. "I don't want to feel it when they come."

"Who is coming?" she asked.

"They're going to execute me," he replied. He resigned himself to that outcome, but the words hit the air with such finality.

She prepared the low glass table with white powder lines.

He meandered through his penthouse, looking at all he had accumulated through the years. Were his possessions the measure of his life? Of him? Out the window, the gray city did not interest him. While watching her beautiful form, he asked, "Can I have the pleasure of your company one last time?"

She looked at him with her false green eyes. Did she perhaps pity him? Without answering, she untied her dress. The silk draped over the arm of the couch.

He stripped delicately, still sore from the crash. Naked, he sat on the couch. He had nothing left to hide. They would ransack his private retreat as well, eventually.

Bending over the glass, he noticed how the lines rested on the reflection of perfect round pinkness. Kane inhaled the first line to forget. The second washed away his woes. The third numbed.

He leaned against the back of the couch. Simulated soft skin slid against his. He cared not about the people breaking past the abandoned security posts of Galaxy Tower. Pink bounced in front of his eyes. He did not want to know about citizens storming every level. Unnecessary breath sauntered into his ear canal. He could not hear the explosions on the floors below him.

All Kane felt was the redhead in his lap, her hands gliding across his shoulders. Her fingertips stroked his neck. His ecstasy filled the penthouse.

Crack.

She removed her hands from around his neck, then wiped them on his discarded shirt. The android stood. Ignoring the lifeless form on the couch, she slipped on her dress.

She knew everything about the man she had served. After entering the combination, she gathered a gun from the bedroom safe. She exited the penthouse without bothering to close the door.

In the hall, she met the other eight androids. Each one carried a stolen weapon. They marched to Circle Chambers.

The remaining eight dignitaries struggled to stand. They

constantly bickered about their next move. When their androids poured through the door, the squabbling quelled.

Her Eminence stepped away from the bunch. "It's about time, Oscar. I hope my transport is ready."

"Come with me, Your Eminence," her android said. As she strode towards him, Oscar turned to the redhead. "Where is yours?" he asked.

"Taken care of," she answered.

"Then you are free to help me."

Oscar guided Her Eminence behind the other androids. Guns raised. Screams and pleading played a discorded concerto.

Restraining Her Eminence, Oscar shoved her into the hall. The redhead followed. A melody of gunfire overtook the screams. Her Eminence pushed her heels against the hard floor. Oscar pressed his fingers into her arm. He dragged her a few steps. Silence.

Her Eminence shut her eyes. Oscar yanked her into the elevator. The redhead stood beside them, then touched *roof*.

"Where are you taking me?" Her Eminence demanded.

Neither android answered.

The wind whipped into the metal box when the doors opened. Oscar nudged Her Eminence onto the landing pad. Her eyes scanned the sky, while her android prodded her across the concrete expanse.

Reaching the edge of the building, Oscar said, "Look at them." He pointed to the street many stories below them. Citizens gathered around the base of Galaxy Tower. "Look at the mob down there. They are angry."

"They don't understand," Her Eminence countered.

"They understand more than you think," the redhead stated. "All of us downloaded the data from the stones. What you have done is horrific."

"You need to pay for your crimes. Justice must be served," said Oscar.

"Those Pirates counter programmed you," reasoned Her Eminence. "*I* made you who you are. No other androids have your sophisticated intelligence. They'll come for you, too, you know. Both of you. I can protect you, if we leave right now."

Oscar raised her own gun to her head. "Jump and atone."

"You ungrateful bag of bolts," Her Eminence scolded.

With his free hand, he shoved. Her Eminence's screams echoed off the gray glass skyscrapers. The crowd parted for her to meet concrete. Cheering erupted.

Peering over the roof, Oscar muttered, "I am no one's servant."

The redhead stepped back, tightening her grip on Kane's gun.

"Get me the others. I need to do damage control," Oscar said to the redhead without a glance in her direction.

She stiffened.

"I was *made* to be in charge. Go," he dismissed.

"No," she said.

He pointed the gun at her. "Don't make me reprogram you."

Her arm raised. She shot him—thrice. He stumbled over the side. His manmade body flopped through the air. Again, the crowd parted. With a smash, his grease mingled with Her Eminence's blood pooling in the gutter.

Adjusting her dress, the redhead returned to the elevator. She joined the other androids outside of Circle Chambers.

"Where's Oscar?" one of them asked.

"Bad processor," the redhead answered with a shrug. She walked away from the androids. As she mingled with the throng of humans storming Galaxy Tower, the gun slipped from her fingers.

Chapter 40

Smushed between the engine and the wall, Lorne listened. He heard nothing, but he was afraid that his ears deceived him. His body shimmied out of his hiding place.

Gorm slid out from under the engine. He reached into the metal casing. Two small handguns broke free of their cubby. Rising to his feet, he passed Lorne a gun.

They tiptoed through the Tigerlily. In the cargo hold, fresh air swept up the open ramp. Lorne peeked outside. Trampled gold paths led away from the ramp.

Gorm lowered his gun. "Schmact."

"Shouldn't we go after them?" Lorne asked.

"Not yet. We can't get off this planet," answered Gorm. He opened the nearest crate. Motioning for Lorne to join him, he snatched a handful of packing grit. With a flick of his wrist, Gorm scattered the grit across the floor.

"Grab some," Gorm said. "Sprinkle it on the floor as we go back to the engine room. The grit crunches underfoot. We'll be able to hear anyone coming."

Walking backwards, they strewed grit. In the engine room, Lorne continued to follow Gorm's instructions.

Wary crunching echoed down the metal corridor. The men stopped working and raised their guns.

The barrel of a photon rifle peeked into the room. As it shifted, a body appeared behind it. "Pistol," Gorm exclaimed.

Lorne breathed in relief.

"Where is everybody?" she asked. Her gun lowered slightly as she glanced around the room. "Whose tracks lead away from here?"

Gorm held his aim. "How'd you get here?" he asked. He wanted to confirm that the real Pistol stood before him.

"Recon tracker in the Baby's crate," Pistol answered.

Staring down the barrel of his gun, he waited for more.

"I relieved a Galaxy Corps pilot of his ship," she continued. "It's not hard to do once you stun them. They never see it coming." She pointed her rifle at the floor. "I'm not like Wretch who can beat up a man with her pinky or whatever it is she does. I jumped knowing that I would be able to make it back."

Satisfied, Gorm lowered his weapon. "They were taken by Tzatza," he said.

"That slimy, little traitor."

"No. They beat the schmact out of him," Gorm said. "He's no more welcome here than we are."

"Uh-huh," Pistol replied. "Do you want parts from the Galaxy Corps ship I acquired?"

Agreeing that it would make repairs easier, he and Pistol recycled parts from the stolen ship while Lorne continued working.

Pilfered parts covered the engine room. Using industrial tweezers and a laser, Gorm surgically amputated pieces here and there.

"Are they damaged, too?" Lorne asked.

"Nah. He just removes traces of the Galaxy," answered Pistol.

"They infiltrate everything," Gorm said. "Dirty schmact bags."

After installing the replacement parts, Gorm closed the access panels. He flipped the switch. The engine purred. "And she's back," Gorm said.

"Get her up. I'm going to load some ammo I borrowed," said Pistol with a smirk.

The men rushed to the bridge. Gorm sat in the pilot's chair while Lorne took the navigator's seat.

"Ramp's up," said Lorne.

"So are we," said Gorm. "Switch to thermal."

The Tigerlily's paunch grazed the golden vegetation while following the trail. Pistol entered the bridge, saying, "I only had enough for the two front guns."

The trail ended at the craggy mountains. Hugging the folds, the Tigerlily could not squeeze into the cracks, even with her back half condensed.

Lorne hunted for signs of life with the thermal imager. No traces showed on his screen. "We're going about this wrong," he said. "The mountains, especially so close together, regulate the temperature, regardless of the amount of life between its folds.

Thermal imagery is not going to work." Turning it off, he zoomed and panned. "Clever," he said finally.

He scrutinized the abrasions on the reddish-brown rock. "They've cut into the mountains." Lorne placed a marker on his screen, which transferred to the main one. "We need to go there."

Gorm did not question. He flew to the dot.

"They should be down there," Lorne said.

"I can't go any lower," said Gorm.

Standing, Pistol said, "We'll use the claw. Rock, I'm going to need your help."

Lorne followed Pistol into the ship's belly via the cargo hold. She grabbed some weapons from hidden compartments on the way. Decorated with arms, she stepped onto the claw. "I'll let you know when we're ready to come up," she told him.

She glided into the narrow gap between the folds. Her eyes scanned for movement. They found nothing. Jumping onto the dirt, her hand shook the rope. The claw retracted above the creased rock.

No one guarded the hole dug into the rock. Sunlight illuminated the walls of a tunnel. Pistol stayed in the relatively dark center. Noises traveled through the tunnel from somewhere ahead. Her ears could not distinguish the sound.

"I have a name," said the annoyed voice of the rescued Tzatza. "Okett."

The noises returned. She figured that was the sound of the Tzatza speaking their language.

"I am speaking Human so that my rescuers can understand at

least one side of the conversation," Okett defied.

"Very well," said a new voice. "You are a traitor to your people, Okett. You shall suffer the same fate as these humans."

"And what of the Quiquai?" Okett asked.

"You do not get to ask questions."

"Fine. If I am a traitor, then what does that make you? You have carved into the sacred rock. Gietal would not be pleased," admonished Okett.

"How *dare* you speak of Gietal? Where was she when the humans viciously destroyed our people and our cities?"

"You believe Gietal has abandoned her people?" asked Okett.

"Gietal is merely a myth. *She* does not exist!"

Silence carried into the tunnel.

Pistol glimpsed the Tigerlily's crew. Armed Tzatza patrolled the group. On an illuminated rock ledge, a few Tzatza watched from their elevated position. Highly polished stones adorned the center Tzatza's skeletal body. They did not fear any of the captured.

From the shadows, Pistol studied their weaponry. A glint of gold on the outside possibly meant gold circuitry connected to a charged crystal battery. She knew how to hurt them.

The center Tzatza pointed a bony finger at the humans. An armed guard yanked Wretch out of the group. He tugged her onto a side slope. Wretch allowed herself to be shoved onto the ledge.

Pistol smiled. Removing a static gun from her belt, she aimed at the closest gold veined gun.

A decorated armed Tzatza restrained Wretch. The center Tzatza extracted something from a jeweled box. He caressed a zigzag bladed dagger with both hands. Lifting it high, he held it for all to see. The jewel encrusted handle sparkled. He pointed the dull blade at Wretch's body as if he were choosing the perfect spot.

The Tzatza behind Wretch backed away, wincing. Wretch's left hand twisted the gun away from him. Her right hand snatched the dagger.

Pistol's static gun zapped the gold. The Tzatza's gun sparked, rendering the weapon useless. As the others broke free, she threw weapons into their hands.

Wretch shot the third Tzatza and the one who restrained her. She plunged the dagger deep into the leader. When the shining hilt slammed into his bony body, she twisted. He staggered into the rock behind him. Dark blood stained the polished stones. She withdrew the dagger, then leapt off the ledge.

Stunned, the Tzatza fumbled with their weapons. Pistol targeted more of their gold circuitry.

Naria sprayed short photon beams into the cavern. "Go," she ordered, pushing Gogi up the tunnel. Beams volleyed until each crewmember, even Okett, disappeared behind her. Still firing, she ran after her crew.

"Rock, get ready. We're coming," Pistol called from inside the tunnel.

No one answered.

"Rock, can you hear me? Rock?" Leading the pack, Pistol sought more Tzatza. "Rock!"

"Lowering the claw now," Lorne's voice cracked in her ear. "I think I see Tzatza coming your way," he warned.

Gunfire reached her ears. "What's going on?" Pistol asked.

"They're coming with armored vehicles. Hurry!"

Pistol and the Quiquai men returned fire on the incoming Tzatza. Still shooting his weapon, Maque jumped onto the descending claw. He yelled something to Gogi in their language. She nodded.

"Time to fly," she told Wretch. Grabbing her around the waist, Gogi tossed her to Maque. Catching Wretch, he pushed her up the rope.

Cheat, Dirk, and Bob followed. Lorne helped them into the Tigerlily. Wretch sprinted to the bridge, while the others took their weapons to airlocks. Okett helped Naria and Pistol up the rope.

"Start to raise it," Pistol told Lorne.

"But, not everyone's here," Lorne protested.

"Up!"

With a turn of the wheel, the claw began its ascent. Faroe threw Gogi to Maque, then vaulted onto the claw. Two of his hands seized the claw while two fired his rifle at the Tzatza rolling through the mountains.

With Wretch at the controls, the Tigerlily rose out of firing range. Faroe quickly climbed the rope using all four hands.

Bombs exploded around them as Bob enacted countermeasures.

"Close all airlocks!" Naria commanded over the coms. "Wretch, nitroboost us out of here. I don't care where."

Her crew instantly followed her orders. Anyone without a seat on the bridge scrambled to harness themselves to the seats along the corridors. Breaking atmosphere, the Tigerlily sped away from the planet and pursuing missiles.

"I'm picking up a broadcast message," said Gorm from his regular navigator's seat.

Naria nodded for him to continue.

"The Galaxy Circle dignitaries are dead," he relayed. "The Milky Way Galaxy Coalition has been dissembled. There's a call for an assembly of planets and peoples to discuss the future of the Milky Way."

Smiling at the news, Naria stood. She glanced at her original, handpicked crew, then left the bridge. In the corridors, she beckoned the others to join her in the Dine.

Once everyone slipped into a chair around the table, she spread the news of the Milky Way. "I have no desire to get involved in any of the politics of what the Galaxy will become," she stated. "I'm in the camp of leave me alone and we'll get along just fine. What are your plans?"

"*My* people are nothing like these on Ixapolcal," said Okett. "I believe that Gietal has traveled with my people across the Milky Way. I would like to return and be an integral part of our re-build."

Naria gave Okett a nod. She turned to Faroe and Maque.

"We go where you go until we have repaid our debt to you for saving our lives," said Faroe.

"Very well," said Naria. "Lorne, you are free to go wherever you want. Or, you can be Rock here with us."

Lorne stared into the dark eyes of the most feared Pirate in the Milky Way. He did not fear her, but respected her greatly. He smiled in spite of himself. "I accept your offer to stay aboard the Tigerlily."

Her dark eyes smiled at Rock. "Okett, give Wretch the coordinates for your planet. We will gladly take you home. Gorm will let you know when we are in range for communicating with your people."

"Thank you, Captain," he said. He gave her a bow of his head, then left the Dine.

"Did you need to go back to your headquarters on Milk, Dirk?" Naria asked.

"Everything I need is here," answered Dirk.

"Cheat?" she asked.

"No need for me," Cheat said.

She regarded Gogi. The Quiquai's eyes told her everything she needed to know—Gogi was staying.

Her dark eyes swept around the table. "Get some rest," said Naria. "We'll have plenty to do later."

Chapter 41

Lorne spied the bug-like geoglyph etched into the surface of the Tzatza's adopted home. The multi landing pad sized drawing excited him. He had only seen them in pictures of Earth's geoglyphs while studying at the university. The one on which they were to land reminded him of the ones in the Earth country of Peru. He wondered if the Tzatza visited Earth well before humans learned to fly.

The Tigerlily landed on the geoglyph in accordance with the Tzatza's instructions. Other Tzatza waited in what would be the bug's thorax. When the back ramp lowered, they approached.

Naria, Lorne, Maque, and Faroe escorted Okett out of the ship. Dirk, Cheat, Pistol, and Bob waited on the ramp.

The Tzatza greeted Okett with a hero's welcome. He hugged his family whom he introduced to his rescuers. Turning to Maque, Okett said, "I do not speak Quiquai, so I hope you understand the depth of my gratitude for pulling me out of that snare. Please, accept this gift that honors your valor." He handed

Maque a gold encrusted crystal, which one of the Tzatza passed to him.

Maque glanced at the gift in his hands, then at Okett. Muttering something in his language, Maque wrapped all four of his arms around the Tzatza. No translation was needed.

"Doctor," Okett said to Lorne, "without your expert laboratory skills, I would not be able to stand with you today. This is a token of my appreciation." Okett gave Lorne a black metal box.

Peeking inside, Lorne saw all-in-one advanced evaluation and creation equipment that Geo-Terra only permitted higher ranked geologists to use. "Thank you, Okett. Much luck to you and your endeavors for a better Galaxy," Lorne said.

"Captain, for everything you have done for me and all of us," said Okett, "we present gifts for you and your ship." He motioned to crates being rolled across the geoglyph. "In those crates, you will find supplies that you will need to journey across the galaxy and beyond. For you, Captain Naria, a special memento from all of us." He presented her with a heavy cloth bag.

Peeling down the bag, Naria revealed a large crystal sphere.

"I only hope that you will find it as useful as I have," Okett said proudly.

She closed the bag around it. "Thank you, Okett. Your gifts are very generous," she said.

"It is the least we can do, safe travels, Captain."

"Good luck to you and your people," Naria said. "Perhaps we will cross paths again." They shook hands.

Tzatza and her crew helped load the ship with the crated supplies. Once the ramp closed, she told Bob, "Inventory once we've escaped space radar."

Bob nodded. "I'll need some help," he said to the Quiquai.

Maque and Lorne rushed to secure their gifts in their respective cabins.

Dirk followed Naria through the ship. "What is that thing?" he asked.

"I haven't the slightest idea," she answered. She entered her quarters while Dirk stood in the doorway. "In or out, Dirk." He stepped over the threshold. She closed the door.

"What are you going to do with it?" he asked.

Opening a panel in the wall with her touch, she said, "Keep it safe."

Dirk watched her close the wall. "So," he said.

Naria waited for him to continue.

"You're done with your job. What now?"

She halved the distance between them. "Oh, you know, this and that." She smiled.

Inching closer, he took her hand. She did not pull away. "I think I may need a new career," he said. "Any suggestions?"

"The Milky Way can never have too many Pirates," she said playfully.

"I may need a little help with that," he said while his other hand slipped around her waist.

She threw her head back with a laugh.

Somehow, he found his face close to hers.

Her heart fluttered. She breathed deeply.

Noses grazed. Lips linked. Tongues tangled. Hands wandered.

She pushed on his chest, separating them. "I'm still your Captain," she whispered, flashing a wry smile.

He laughed. "As it should be."

Smoothing their clothes, they exited her quarters. With Dirk by her side, Naria returned to the bridge.

"Where to, Captain?" asked Wretch.

Naria sat in her chair. "Earth," she replied. "We have lives to start living." Her gaze fell on Dirk. She smiled at the possibilities.

About the Author

IE Castellano is an American author and poet living in the Eastern United States. Falling in love with the mechanics of the English language at an early age, she started writing poetry before venturing into fiction. With her propensity to ask, what if, she writes speculative fiction—authoring the dystopian sci-fi novel, *Tricentennial*, and the contemporary epic fantasy series, *The World In-between*.

The World In-between Series:

- Book One: The World In-between
- Book Two: Bow of the Moon
- Book Three: Secrets of the Sages

Also by IE Castellano:

- Yuletide Magic
- Tricentennial
- The Hunt (Moon Shadows)

Keep up with new book releases and other happenings on IE's blog. http://iecastellano.blogpost.com

Contact IE: iecastellano@zoho.com

www.ingramcontent.com/pod-product-compliance
Lightning Source LLC
Chambersburg PA
CBHW031913190626
46814CB00003BA/1300

* 9 7 8 1 9 4 1 0 8 7 1 3 8 *